DARK FAERIE

ALFHEIM ACADEMY: BOOK TWO

S.T. BENDE

To my little explorers.

CHAPTER 1

RULING A REALM WAS never going to be easy. I wasn't stupid. I'd known taking on this job at this time would create an unfathomable amount of stress. Everyone from my aunt to my friends to the queen herself had told me as much.

As the crown princess of Alfheim, my duties consisted of co-ruling with a grandmother whose inability to job-share was a living nightmare, fighting the queen's monster minister of state on *every single freaking point*, and trying to convince our tyrannical cabinet members to do literally anything good. Ever. On top of ruling our hot mess of a kingdom, I was supposed to be finishing my third year at Alfheim Academy, acing my final exams, and preparing for a formal dinner with a visiting royal family who thought we were the cosmos' biggest idiots. *Because we were.*

This was *so* not what I'd signed up for.

"The next matter on our agenda is tomorrow's state

dinner." My grandmother's prim voice cut through my mental chatter.

I forced myself out of my head by focusing on the shiny, lacquered floor of Queen Constance's office. Like everything else in the royal residence, it was polished to perfection. In front of me, Constance's ornately carved desk sparkled beneath the glistening chandelier. And her smudge-free floor-to-ceiling windows overlooked gardens that were somehow *always* in bloom. Did the gardeners perform nightly replants? As scary as Constance was, I wouldn't put it past them.

"You are to meet me in my drawing room fully dressed at five o'clock tomorrow evening." Constance's shimmering wings fluttered lightly behind her as she leaned forward in her chair. Like me, she was an *älva*—a faerie. "I shouldn't have to say this, but in light of last week's incident, I'm compelled to remind you that you *must* wear an appropriate gown. Also, appropriate footwear," she added when I opened my mouth. "No combat boots."

Heat crept along my neck.

"That briefing said we were going to a swordsman-ship demonstration," I muttered. "I thought I'd be participating."

"You were not," the queen said stiffly. "And you looked silly sitting in the royal box, dressed for sport."

Obviously.

"Vendya will personally dress Aura for tomorrow's

event." Our protocol advisor, Eunice, chimed in. "I'll confirm her fitting after this meeting."

"Excellent." Constance stared at me. "Do I need to impress upon you the importance of this dinner?"

I bit back the reply that danced on my tongue. This state dinner with Vanaheim's royal family would be our first in seventeen years—since before Constance had created the blockade that kept off-worlders from entering our realm. The Alfheim Barrier had caused a *lot* of discord, and this was the first step in mending fences . . . and in asking for help rebuilding our world. We'd done plenty of damage since Narrik had taken over as minister of state, and our leaders could learn a lot from Vanaheim's. *If they're even willing to teach us.*

"Aura?" Constance arched her brow.

"No," I said quietly. "You don't need to explain. I know what a big deal this is."

"I'm glad," Constance said. "With our *Opprør* senators still missing, it's more important than ever that you align yourself with influential leaders. Particularly those whose values mirror your own."

Eunice shifted in the chair beside me, crossing her feet at the ankles as she passed me a leather-bound packet. "This is our most current briefing on Vanaheim's royal family. It should tell you everything you need to know about their political and personal histories. It also provides conversational points pertaining to private interests, from sport to art to literature. It will behoove you to memorize its contents in advance of tomorrow's dinner."

I weighed the massive booklet in one hand. "This briefing is intense, Eunice. Even for you."

My advisor ducked her head. "Thank you."

It hadn't been a compliment.

"That reminds me." My grandmother turned to our advisor. "Prepare a briefing for Aura on the customs and procedures pertaining to our dealings with the meadow elves. They've requested a meeting regarding the deterioration of the eastern poppy fields, and I'd like Aura to chair the response."

Eunice opened the gilded notebook she always carried. "Of course."

"You'd like me to do what now?" I shifted my focus from Eunice's sparkly calendar.

"On account of our . . . tenuous relationship with the colonies near Meina," Constance began.

"You mean Meina, the town your minster of state torched to quell a much-deserved rebellion? *That* Meina?"

"Crown Princess." Eunice tutted. "Show some decorum."

"I stated a fact," I pointed out. "Last year, Fyrs Narrik lit up a town because its citizens challenged him. People died. This is not news."

"Regardless." Eunice shook her head. "It would behoove you to exercise diplomacy in *all* dealings—including those with your queen."

"My co-regent. We've had equal responsibilities for what, half a year now? Feels longer," I muttered as I turned back to Constance. "So, let me guess—these meadow elves were adversely affected by the fire?"

"Correct." Constance glanced at a piece of paper on her desk. "A portion of their fields have stopped producing, which caused the death of a . . . worm species, I believe. Which caused the avians who cross-pollenated their crops to evacuate. Which has led to the —how did they put it? 'Complete collapse of their ecological infrastructure.'"

My eyes widened. "What have we done to fix it?"

"To date, it looks like . . ." Constance scanned the paper. "Nothing."

"Seriously?" I reached across the desk and ripped the page from Constance's bony hand.

"Crown Princess!"

"Sorry, not sorry, Eunice." I scanned the document. "Jeez. That fire was nine months ago. This says it's their fifth time requesting a meeting. Have we just been ignoring them?"

Constance raised her chin. "The crown has many pressing matters."

"Uh-huh," I said drily. "So, you're passing this one off to me?"

Constance straightened her spine against the embroidered pillow lining her chair. "Eunice, send word to the meadow elves they shall have their meeting with the Crown Princess on Saturday. She will personally hear their grievances."

"As you wish, Your Majesty." Eunice's ruby finger-nails gripped her pen. Her unnaturally tidy script filled the page of her notebook. "Will the rest of the cabinet be joining her?"

Blood rushed from my face. "The rest of the—wait. What?"

"Only the senior members." Constance drummed her fingertips against the polished wood of her desk.

"Hold on." I raised my hand. "The senior members of your cabinet are Narrik, and three of his goons."

"Language," Eunice tutted.

"Goons isn't a bad word!"

"It's a word unbecoming of royalty. It would behoove you to act *and speak* as the co-regent you are, at *all* times."

Again with the behoove-ing. If Eunice said that word one more time, I would offer to tattoo it to her forehead.

"Fine. I'm not on great terms with the senior members of your cabinet—or any of your cabinet, actually." It was true. Constance's cabinet had remained unchanged, despite our new job-share. They were pro-Narrik, pro-government control, and *extremely* anti-me. Plus, they'd been the ones who caused the fire the meadow elves had suffered from in the first place. "Can't I just take the meeting alone?"

"Our bylaws prohibit it." Eunice shook her head. Her bun was so tight, her hair didn't move at all. "I understand you have found working with the existing cabinet to be difficult."

Cue the understatement police.

"But rules are rules. And Alfheim has operated as it

is for centuries. A regent simply does not take a meeting alone. The precedent it would set . . ." Eunice shuddered.

I sighed. "So, it's me, Narrik, and the goons—yes, I am calling them goons—taking the meeting. When will it be?"

"Saturday afternoon, at two." Constance paged through the calendar on her desk. Though the rest of us used data pads, she and Eunice clung to the organizational system they'd developed decades ago. "It's the first date the cabinet members will be free. Usually I do not ask them to work that late in the week, but seeing as they will be breaking for their summer recess the following Monday, they should cede my request."

"*Perfekt.*" I mentally added *meet with jerky cabinet members on first day of summer vacation* to my to-do list.

Who said being a princess isn't fun?

My gaze caught on the framed portrait of Queen Constance's cabinet. In it, the ten members stood proudly on the steps of the senate building. Although we were a monarchy, the regent carried only one-third of the realm's decision-making authority. The other thirds went to the cabinet and the senate, respectively. Which meant that the ten jerks in the picture carried enormous power—a fact they held over our heads daily.

"Hey." I turned back to Constance. "Any chance we're going to get to swap out some of those cabinet members for ones who actually like me? *Ever?*"

"That would require a vote," Eunice reminded me.

"And with the *Opprør* senators still missing, it is highly unlikely their *Kongelig* counterparts would unseat members of their own party."

I gritted my teeth. "I had to ask."

Eunice shot me a sympathetic look. She'd seen my grandmother through the early years of her reign. She'd never admit it, but she'd been hurt that Constance had allowed the realm to fall into chaos. I supposed it was why she was so tough on me. I was her do-over—her chance to guide a more progressive, less tyrannical regent at the start of her time on the throne. And, hopefully, shape a brighter future for our realm.

Too bad Alfheim's political structure gave me basically *zero* authority.

"Are we finished?" Constance made a mark on her calendar. "I have a luncheon to attend."

"And I have a final exam." I stood. "I'm good here, right?"

"Let me just confirm your regent schedule, Princess." Eunice glanced at her notebook. "On Saturday, you'll meet with the meadow elves and the senior cabinet members at the senate building. I'll message a briefing to you no later than dinnertime tonight. The state dinner will be held tomorrow, here at the royal residence. I'll have the seamstress stop by your dormitory this evening for your fitting. Afterwards, she will coordinate with your date on his ensemble."

Right. Let's add try on dresses *to the week's crazy.*

"Regarding your academics, your *Verge* final is—"

"Soon." I glanced at the clock on Constance's office wall. "It's soon, so if we could wrap this up—"

"It will behoove you to hear your *complete* schedule," Eunice said primly.

Fourth time's a charm. Behoove tattoo time!

Snort.

"Fine. Lay it on me." I crossed my arms, mentally running through the combat sequences I'd have to execute for that afternoon's test.

"Your *Empati* exam is tomorrow morning, followed by your History of Alfheim exam in the afternoon. I trust you have remained on top of your studies this semester?"

"Of course." I nodded at Eunice. "But if you don't let me go soon, I'll flunk *Verge* on account of absenteeism."

Eunice turned her torso to Constance. "I am finished with the crown princess if you are."

"Go." My grandmother flicked her wrist. "Score well. Bring glory to the crown."

She had the weirdest way of saying good luck.

"Okay. See you guys, uh . . . tomorrow night, I guess."

"At the state dinner," Eunice reminded me.

"Yep. And I will be totally prepared. I promise." I picked up my books and the Vanaheim briefing, and backed slowly out of the room. "Have fun with your —oof!"

Breath whooshed from my lungs as my spine struck something hard. My balance unhinged and I stumbled forward, spilling the contents of my arms on the ground. I dropped to a knee to retrieve my belongings. As I did, I caught sight of narrow black boots in my periphery. They were so shiny, I was able to catch my surprised reflection in their well-kept depths.

Skit. What's he *doing here?*

"The princess has fallen." Minister Narrik's cold voice broke the silence. I slid my gaze upward, taking in his all-black ensemble of neatly pressed slacks, and his fitted military jacket, and a cap that he'd placed atop his slightly-too-small head. "Whatever shall we do?"

"Help me up, for starters." I retrieved my gear, and pushed myself to my feet.

"I wouldn't want to interfere with your . . . independence." Narrik looked down his narrow nose at me.

"No." My knuckles whitened as I gripped my books. "It's not like you to interfere with things."

Narrik's nostrils flared. He arched one brow, no doubt intending to launch into whatever tirade he was riding that day. But before he could speak, Eunice's head shake caught my eye.

"Do not engage," she mouthed. *"Please."*

Fine.

I drew a slow breath, and turned toward the exit. Without another word, I marched through the door. When I was outside Constance's office, Narrik chuckled.

"Leave us, Eunice," he said quietly. "The queen and I have things to discuss."

"I don't have you on my agenda." My grandmother's voice trembled over the final word. Was she . . . *afraid?*

"Well, you are on mine." Narrik's words carried a hint of a threat. "Leave us, Eunice. Now."

"Yes, minister." Eunice's footsteps scurried across the polished floor. I slowed my steps as the door clicked closed behind me. When I turned around, I caught my advisor's worried look.

"What's that about?" I whispered.

"It's not my place to ask. Nor is it yours. Don't you have an exam to attend?" She ran a hand along her graying hairline.

"I do." And Alfheim Academy was a solid twenty minute's jog from the royal residence. But for this, I'd cut it close.

I inched toward the door, and pressed my ear to the wall.

"Crown Princess," Eunice admonished.

"Shh!" I held a finger to my lips. "I'm regent-ing."

"Absolutely not." Narrik's angry voice pierced the quiet. "As far as I am concerned, this matter was resolved weeks ago. I won't be addressing it again."

Eunice's brows knitted together in worry.

"I am your regent." Constance's pitch betrayed her frustration. "And as an appointed member of my cabinet, you would do well to—"

"What I'll do well, *Your Majesty*, is exactly what you brought me on to do—keep the wolves at bay. At least for a little while longer."

"What does that mean?" Constance asked.

Sharp footsteps moved toward the door. I stepped

back as it opened just enough for me to catch Narrik's hushed threat.

"Need I remind you how easy it would be to replace a monarch?"

Eunice's sharp inhale pulled my attention from the door. With her wide eyes and white-knuckled grip on her notebook, the woman perfectly reflected my own feelings. What the Helheim was going on between Constance and Narrik? And why was the queen letting *anyone* talk to her like that?

As I debated whether to burst in and defend my grandmother's dubious honor, the door opened fully and Narrik slipped through. He paused briefly as he passed me, his cold, soulless stare holding me in its icy grip. My insides clenched. Was I the monarch he intended to replace? *Right then?*

But he kept walking, moving down the hall in clipped strides until his figure disappeared around the corner.

When he was gone, I turned to Eunice in shock. "What. The. Actual. Helheim?"

Narrik's hold on Constance had never made sense. When I'd asked her to replace him as minister of state with literally anyone else, she'd claimed doing so would violate constitutional protocol. But after what I'd just heard, perhaps her thinking was grounded in something less . . . governmental. Maybe the reason Constance kept Narrik on the payroll was because he had something over her.

My eyes narrowed at the open door. It was time to find out what Granny dearest was hiding.

I marched determinedly into the queen's office. "Constance," I demanded. "What was that about? If there's something you're not telling me, so help me Frigga, I'll—oh, my gods. Are you all right?" My anger dissipated as I ran to her side.

The queen's normally pale skin was ghostly white, and lined with a thin sheen of sweat. Her hands shook, and her wings, usually ramrod straight, drooped around her trembling shoulders.

Without another word, I gently guided her into her seat.

"What did he do to you?" Eunice whispered from the doorway.

Constance's head snapped up. "You shouldn't have heard that."

"Well, we did," I pointed out. "And it was awful. Did Narrik threaten to kill you?"

"It's not the first time," Constance said.

I knelt so our eyes were level. "We *have* to get rid of him. We can't have someone like that poisoning the world we're trying to build."

"It's not that simple." Constance sighed. "Fyrs is a threat, yes. He's ambitious and focused, and would gladly take the throne himself if our succession laws were different. But there are worse threats out there. Fyrs, well . . . I'm sure you heard him."

"He keeps the wolves at bay." I frowned. "What wolves? Who's he holding back?"

"Who isn't he holding back?" Constance's laugh was brittle. "All the dark realms want me dead. Half the light realms want me dethroned. In the public's eyes, I'm unredeemable. There's no return from what they perceive I've done to Alfheim—never mind that I did it to keep them alive."

"I know you think you acted for the good of the realm, but even you have to admit, what you did was horrendous."

"If you say so." At Constance's raised chin, I stifled my sigh. Would there *ever* be a day when she saw things as they actually were?

"Why is everyone so afraid of Narrik?" I changed course. "What's he got over them?"

Constance's nostrils flared, and the whites of her eyes widened.

What's he got over you?

"Fyrs has positioned himself advantageously. At the start of his ministry, he befriended key officials and placed them in compromising positions. He then used that collateral to leapfrog into higher posts, finally claiming the minister of state title. Once there, he was able to impose his will through questionable part-nerships."

"What do you mean? Isn't he loyal to Alfheim?"

"Fyrs is loyal to Fyrs. He's never outwardly declared fealty to another realm, but his practices rarely align with the values of this one. Many suspect he has off-realm benefactors. Though of course nothing has ever been confirmed."

My jaw unhinged. "If you think that's true, why haven't you kicked him out?"

"I've told you. The regent does not have the power to unseat high-level ministers. An act of that magnitude would require confirmation by the senate."

"Okay, so why haven't they done it?"

Constance pursed her lips. "I believe they, too, have been compromised."

Jeez. Was the entire government of Alfheim corrupt?

"At some point, we're going to have to do a clean sweep of everyone who votes on anything ever." Frustration roiled in my gut. "Our realm is clearly broken. We restored the crystal, we removed the barrier, and we're working to reinstate merit-based admissions to the academy. But even with all of that, Alfheim's still in crisis. The meadow elves have been trying to get a meeting for five months—*five months*, Constance. Their region is dying, and we've done *nothing* to help them."

"The crown has—"

"I *know* the crown is busy. But what could possibly be more important to us than the needs of our citizens? How have we continued to fail them? And how the Helheim have we not kicked that monster Narrik out of office?"

"Keep your voice down," Constance hissed.

"I don't care if he hears me." I crossed my arms. "I don't care if *anyone* hears me. Things are not right around here. And if nobody else is going to step up, then I will."

"What do you mean by that?"

The gentle chimes of the clock let me know I'd blown well past my welcome. *Crêpes.* "I have an exam to get to."

"Young lady." The queen's pitch rose. "I asked you a question."

"And I told you I have a test. I'll see you at the state dinner. We can talk after that." With a nod at Eunice, who still clung to her notebook like a granny clutching her pearls, I turned on one foot and bolted from the queen's office. I'd have to sprint all the way to the academy if I didn't want to miss my final. And if I did . . .

Not an option. Run faster.

I lowered my head and pumped my legs. My heels kicked up dirt as I barreled along the road that connected the palace and the academy. Nobody had ever said being a student/princess would be easy. But I was determined to do right by my citizens, my realm, and my *Verge* training partner. I wasn't about to let any of them—or myself—down.

CHAPTER 2

"**CUTTING IT PRETTY CLOSE**, huh, Princess?" Viggo nudged me with his shoulder as I slipped into line beside him.

I pointed to the clock that hung to the left of the climbing wall. "I have a full half-minute to spare, thank you very much. And stop calling me that. You know I hate it."

"Whatever you say, *Glitre*." Viggo's dimple popped, and I rolled my eyes. A deep chuckle from my right made me look over, and I grinned at my cousin as he took his place beside me.

Despite growing up on Svartalfheim, Ondyr had settled right in at Alfheim Academy. Within weeks, he'd become one of the stars of the *Verge* program, resumed his easy friendship with Viggo, and managed to steer clear of the hormonal horde of *Styra*—the realm's resident mean girls, who'd made no secret of their desire to stake a claim on him. Instead, he was going to the Solstice Dance with Jande—my *Elementär* friend, who was partial to crystal rings, flowy scarves, and recent Svartalfheim transfers with a wicked sense of humor and a mean right hook.

I'd waited a lifetime to get a cousin. Thank gods he'd turned out to be awesome.

"*Glitre?*" Ondyr arched his brow. "Sorry, I still don't get it."

"Ondyr's later than me." I stared Viggo down. "What do you have to say to him?"

"*Hei*, man." Viggo reached over and rapped his knuckles against his friend's.

"*Hei.*" Ondyr grinned at Viggo. "You ready for today?"

"Readier than she is." Viggo angled his head toward me. "She told me last night she's still having a hard time with the aerial sequence."

"I did not." I glared. "What I said was that I was going to wipe the floor with you on aerials. And you said 'wanna bet,' and I said, 'loser has to take on *Verge* cleaning duty for two weeks,' and *you* said—"

"If you're quite through, we can begin." Aunt Signy marched across the training room. We all snapped to attention, facing the wall of windows with our feet shoulder-width apart and our hands folded behind our backs. Signy paced in front of us, scrutinizing everything from our posture to our uniforms, scribbling notes on her clipboard as she rendered her judgment. I pulled my shoulders taut and stared straight ahead, doing my best to ignore the soft laughter coming from either side of me.

Boys.

"Today's exam will count for a third of your final grade." Signy paused in front of Viggo, and the laughter stopped. "I know how hard all of you have worked, and I hope *you* know how proud Headmistress Herliefer and I are of each and every one of you. The *Verge* discipline is strenuous, and requires the highest standard of physical and mental acuity. Only our top graduates will earn places as *Protektors*, warriors, and members of the royal guard. So, go out there and give this your all. You will have fifteen minutes to warm up. Will that be enough?"

"Yes, Professor Bergen," chorused the class.

"Very good. I want each of you to make *yourselves* proud." Signy dismissed us with a wave, and we hurried to our spots. Since Viggo and I were the only winged *Verge*, we'd been assigned to the outdoor field. There, we'd work on our aerials—a series of evasive maneuvers that ended with an airborne version of a standard hand-to-hand attack. During Sunday's practice, Viggo had outmaneuvered me in seven out of ten sessions.

I was determined to level the score. Two weeks' worth of cleaning duty—not to mention my pride— stood on the line.

"Try not to hurt him too badly," Ondyr called over. He and his training partner, a fiery redhead named Zara, followed us to the field. They each carried a broadsword, which they twirled comfortably as they walked. "We're supposed to rehearse our History of Alfheim presentation after this, and I need him in one piece."

"I can't make any promises." I shrugged.

Zara grinned. "Give him Helheim."

"Thanks." I returned the smile.

"Enough chatting," Signy yelled from inside. "Get to work out there!"

Ondyr and Zara crossed to the far end of the field and drew their blades. They were equally matched in strength and dexterity, though Zara had the advantage of two-and-a half additional years of the academy's stringent training. Ondyr's style was less refined, but he'd quickly adapted to the *Verge* techniques—and managed to find workarounds for sequences that proved difficult for his more aggressive form.

"Aura? We doing this or what?" Viggo's deep voice pulled me back to the field. He'd already popped out his wings, and they now fluttered behind him: two massive silver appendages waving in the early afternoon breeze. My gaze stalled on the sword-shaped mark at the tip of one. It was the mirror image of mine . . . and the telltale sign identifying us as mates. When I'd first discovered the Norns had paired us up *for all of eternity* it had freaked me out. But now—

"Aura?" Viggo repeated.

"Right. Let's go." I fisted my hands and drew my shoulder blades down, releasing my own wings. I flapped twice, rising above the field before calling out. "You coming?"

Viggo's emerald eyes sparkled as he flew toward me. We generally kept our wings under wraps—I was still getting used to having mine, and the academy-issued blazers didn't exactly accommodate additional appendages. But the racerback tank tops we trained in offered more flexibility, and the rare days we ran aerial drills had become my favorites. Flying was *amazing*—and when we paired it with combat drills, it offered an incredible blend of freedom and ferocity.

Plus, Viggo looked *really* good in the air.

"I'm running offensive this time," I declared. "You good with defense?"

"Good enough to win our bet," Viggo goaded.

I narrowed my eyes. "Oh, it's on, Sorenssön. Get ready to get beat. Beaten. Whatever."

It was hard to focus with his arms flexed and his wings flapping.

"On my mark, then." Viggo ran a hand through tousled, chestnut waves. *Not helping.* "Three. Two. One."

"Go!" I called. Viggo darted for the tree line, and I charged after him. He wove in and out of the purple-tipped pines, spinning to avoid a newly bloomed bush before shooting above the forest and heading toward the *Verge* center. I easily kept up with him, making sure to tuck in my wings as I rounded the tree-trunks. I'd learned the hard way how sensitive wings were—and I was determined to not repeat last week's mistake. *Ouch.*

"Incoming," I shouted as I barreled for the field.

Viggo shifted up, throwing out his arm and hooking my elbow so we spiraled toward the grass. We were supposed to simulate a free-fall until the last possible second, then shift into an airborne gamma combat sequence—a series of punch-jabs, followed by round-houses, then front kicks. Whoever stayed in the air the longest would be the winner. They'd earn ten additional points on the final exam, plus bragging rights and a week off cleaning duty.

Viggo was going down.

I released his arm as we ended our free-fall, then threw a sharp right hook at his torso. It struck with enough force to knock him off-balance. As he flailed, I delivered two jabs to his shoulder, pushing him closer to the grass. He recovered as my foot neared his ribs and he reached out, catching my calf mid-kick and wrenching it to the side. I tumbled through the air, flapping fiercely until I'd stopped my spin. Then I launched myself upward and dove, beelining straight for Viggo's back. He turned just as I got close, wrapping his arms around my shoulders and angling his own so we spiraled for the ground.

"We're going to hit!" I shouted. "Let go!"

"You yielding to me, Princess?" Viggo yelled.

"I told you to stop. Calling. Me. That!" I shoved Viggo and shifted, rotating so my knees skimmed the tips of the grass. My partner hit the ground with a loud *thunk*, and I quickly adjusted my trajectory so I flew toward him. I dropped down, straddling him and pinning his neck with my forearm. "Gotcha." I grinned.

Viggo's lazy smile quickened my heartrate. "You still have a few to go to beat my record."

"Three more and then we're even," I reminded him. "And I can *definitely* do that three more times. Four if you keep flying that slow through the trees."

"Bring it," Viggo challenged.

I released his neck and offered my hand, helping him to his feet. As he rose, he tugged me forward so we stood chest to chest. His heart pounded beneath the thin fabric of his tank top, the sensation spiking my own pulse. My breath hitched as Viggo tightened his grip around my hand and leaned in to whisper in my ear, "That was hot, *Glitre*."

My heartrate shot straight through the clouds. Things had been so crazy since I'd become co-regent, we'd barely gotten any time alone together. But being pressed against Viggo, breathing in his familiar mixture of sweat and cedar, his lips moving softly against my ear . . . I turned my head, intending to brush my lips against Viggo's neck. But as I moved, he released my hand and leapt in the air.

"Now do that three more times," he called as he soared straight for the trees.

With a groan, I stretched my wings and took off after him. He was infuriating. And intoxicating. And insufferable. And irresistible.

And I was going to *destroy* him in the next round.

I successfully pinned Viggo five more times before Signy and Headmistress Herliefer evaluated us. My meeting with Constance had left me with a *lot* of pent-up frustration, and I was only too happy to let it out on my training partner. By the time our professors declared me the victor, both Viggo and I were out of breath, covered in mud, and rocking twin pairs of torn pants. We'd steered too close to a tree on one of our descents, and since neither of us had been willing to yield, we'd gotten pretty torn up. But we'd both passed, thank gods. And we had the bruises to show for it.

"Here." I tossed Viggo a towel from the table beside the lawn. "Sorry I was so rough on you. Actually, I'm not sorry. I really wanted a break from cleaning duty."

"Obviously." Viggo wiped the mud from his face. "So, what happened out there? Did I do something to upset you or what?"

"It's not you." I traded my dirt-covered towel for a fresh one and used it to wring mud from the end of my braid. "It's my grandmother. And Narrik. And, well, everything."

"Explain." Viggo grabbed a clean towel and dabbed at a cut on his leg.

"You, me, and our friends . . . we did everything we were supposed to." I sat on the grass and shifted into a hamstring stretch. "We found the missing crystal and restored it to the Alfheim Tree, but the realm's still filled with darkness—there's a lot of pain left over from the cruelty Narrik's spread over the years. We convinced Constance to make me the co-regent, but the *Kongelig* still control the cabinet and the senate, so we can't actually push any of our changes through. And, in spite of *everything* we've worked for, Alfheim's still dying."

"How so?" Viggo dropped onto the grass beside me.

"I found out today the meadow elves have been trying to get someone from the capital to meet with them for months. Their ecosystem's collapsing—residual effects from that fire Narrik set in Meina. And that was one of his smaller acts of destruction. Frigga only knows what the rest of the realm is facing in the aftermath of his tyranny. But I don't have time to think about that, much less fix it, because I have to behave with *decorum* while the monster who caused this whole mess in the first place runs my cabinet. I've got to memorize an insane number of facts about Vanaheim's royal family *in a day*, then play nice with everyone who expects me to be just as bad at running things as my grandmother was. Oh, and I have two more finals to not fail."

Frustration colored my vision, and I flopped backward on the grass and blinked at the clouds.

"Wow." Viggo wrapped his hand around mine. "That is one lousy week."

"You're telling me," I muttered.

"Hey, I get that you're frustrated." He slung his towel around his neck and lay on his back beside me. "It's been a *lot* to take in, month after month."

Preach.

"But you're not in this alone. You and I are a team,

Glitre. After tomorrow's exams and the state dinner, and we'll figure it out. I promise."

"The realm shouldn't be this broken," I whispered. "Not after all of this time."

"It shouldn't." Viggo reached over to cup my chin between his thumb and pointer finger. "We'll get to the bottom of this—fix whatever's wrong with Alfheim. *Together.*"

"Thanks," I whispered.

"Right after we get through this week."

Gulp

"So?" Ondyr's cheerful tenor echoed across the field. "Who won?"

"Aura." Viggo squeezed my hand. He shot me a wink before sitting. "Barely."

"Hugely," I corrected as I let him pull me up after him.

"I'm not surprised." Zara grabbed a towel and came to join us. "Aura's more fluid in the air than Viggo. If he released earlier in his free-spin, he could catch her off-balance and—"

"Hey!" I frowned. "Don't help him!"

"I'm helping both of you. You deserve a better opponent. It'll give you a greater chance of survival if . . ."

Zara didn't have to finish. If Alfheim was attacked again. If the missing *Opprør* never returned. If the *Kongelig* kept stonewalling our proposals, and we had to forcibly enact peace. There were so many ifs dangling out there. And the scariest of all . . .

What if things never get better?

"Hey." Ondyr reached over to cuff me on the arm. "No long faces. This exam's over. Now we just have to not fail History of Alfheim and it's hello, summer vacation."

"That one's half of our final grade." I exhaled. "No pressure."

"None at all." Ondyr shuddered. "One more night of chaos . . ."

"For you guys." I turned to Viggo. "I forgot. The seamstress needs to see you about your outfit for the state dinner. She'll swing by your place after she's done with me tonight."

"Aw, Viggo." Ondyr beamed. "You get a gown, too?"

Viggo rolled his eyes good-naturedly. "Something like that."

Zara wrapped her arms around her knees. "Try not to stress, you guys. This week will be over soon enough, and then everything will go back to normal."

My fingers tightened around Viggo's, and I bit on my bottom lip.

That's what I'm afraid of.

"**A**URA? THANK GODS YOU'RE** home. I'm so sorry. I couldn't get her to leave and, well . . . get in here."

Dinner had been a subdued affair, and Elin and I had just returned from the dining hall. Now we exchanged worried looks as we pushed through the door of our suite.

"Finna?" I asked cautiously. "Are you all right?"

"I'm fine." Finna's voice carried the too-high edge of someone experiencing . . . was that guilt?

"Who couldn't you get to leave?" Elin called. "Do we need to call for security, or—"

"Oh, my gods." My hand flew to my mouth as I rounded the corner. My roommate stood atop a small box, swathed from head to toe in layers of filmy, plum-colored tulle. Her hair was twisted in an ornate crown of braids, and she wore a gown that nipped in at her waist before fluttering delicately downward and flaring at her calves. She twirled experimentally as we entered, her mocha skin pinked with either excitement or embarrassment.

Maybe both?

"Sorry," she whispered. "But Vendya said she had an extra dress that might fit me for the Solstice Dance. I guess she made a few for you for your state dinner, but decided this one wasn't right for your complexion. And when she saw our waists were similar in size . . ."

Beside me, Elin's shoulders trembled with barely contained laughter.

"Don't apologize." I raised my hand. "It's perfect."

"It looks *beautiful* on her." Vendya clapped her hands together. The royal seamstress was a tall, thin woman who carried herself with the grace I now recognized as a job requirement for those employed by my grandmother. "Much lovelier than it would have been on Princess Aura."

"Hey," Elin objected.

But I shook my head. "No, it's true. I could never pull off that shade. Or that cut. It's definitely made for you."

"Thanks." Finna flushed.

"Sorry. I should have warned you about Vendya coming over. Actually, sorry to you, Vendya—I kind of forgot."

Vendya placed her hands on her hips. "You forgot you had an appointment with the most sought-after seamstress in the realm?"

"In all fairness, it's been kind of a day."

Vendya's frown let me know my excuse carried no weight. "Since you were late, I found your escort and took his measurements."

"Viggo's getting an outfit too?" Elin asked.

"Some kind of a suit for the dinner, I think. Right?" I turned to Vendya.

"Some kind of suit? Do you know *anything* about fashion? He will be wearing an ensemble perfectly tailored to complement yours. Obviously."

"Uh, right." I bit the inside of my cheek. *Yikes.*

"Are you sure it's okay for me to wear this?" Finna piped up. "I know you made it for Aura, and I don't want to upset Queen Cons—"

"It is yours." Vendya folded her hands together and bowed deeply.

Finna shot me a curious look before mimicking the gesture. "Well, okay then. Thank you." She lifted her skirt and stepped towards the bathroom. "It's a *lot* nicer than the one I picked out."

"I should hope so." Vendya huffed.

"It's gorgeous. Truly one of a kind." I meant it. But I also wanted to unruffle Vendya's feathers. "So . . . what do you need me to do?"

"You." Vendya pointed at Elin. "What size are you?"

"Excuse me?" My friend arched her brows.

"Never mind." Vendya waggled her finger. "You are the *Musa, ja?*"

"Um, *ja.*" Elin shrugged. "Why?"

"I have another design. Now I realize that pattern

will be too busy for the crown princess. But it might work for you. Go. Try on the pink garment bag."

"Oh, I'm not really a pink kind of gi—"

"Try it on!" Vendya snapped.

"Okay! Sorry!" Elin scooped up the bag and scurried into the bathroom. Finna followed her in with wide eyes.

"She's scary," my friend muttered.

"No *skit*," Elin mumbled back.

"I can hear you!" Vendya shouted. Then she turned to me with a serene smile. "Now, Aura. Tell me a bit about yourself."

"I, uh . . ." I eyed the five remaining garment bags on my bed. "I'm not that into dresses. Or formalities. Or fancy dinners, so I'll take whichever one of those is the most comfortable . . . and if it could have pockets, that'd be great."

Vendya's eyes narrowed. "Why wouldn't it have pockets?"

Exactly.

Vendya walked a slow circle around me, holding her hands as if she was framing a film shot. After an eternity, she stepped closer, pinching my braid between two fingers and squinting at the strands. I held my breath as she leaned into my face and stared at my eyes. Either she was working out my coloring, or she was trying to scare the *skit* out of me.

Maybe she was doing both.

"The ivory," she finally declared.

"Excuse me?"

"The ivory ballgown. In chiffon. *That* is the one for you."

Oh, gods. She'd said ballgown.

"Is there maybe one that's more of a, I don't know, more fitted cut than a—"

"Try it on!" Vendya barked.

Double yikes.

"Which bag is it?"

"Stand on the box," Vendya ordered. "Take off those horrid school clothes. When will they allow me to design more *flattering* ensembles for our future leaders?"

"If by flattering you mean *not* khaki and pleats, I'm all over it. Just tell me who I have to talk to."

"Why are you still not undressed?" Vendya lifted one of the garment bags from my bed and placed it on top of the others. I slipped out of my blazer and skirt while she unzipped the bag and withdrew a creamy chiffon confection far fancier than anything I'd ever seen. Its fitted bodice dipped to a low *V* at the waist, then pooled into a voluminous skirt that looked like it contained a solid hundred yards of fabric. Delicate yellow and blue flowers were embroidered along the skirt, with a matching strand atop the dress's sweetheart neckline. A light layer of mesh made up the sleeves and top of the bodice, affording the illusion of straplessness, while maintaining what I had no doubt was the queen's rigorous standard of modesty. It was beautiful. Regal.

And totally not me.

"Arms up," Vendya ordered. I raised my arms and allowed her to slide the dress over my head. Once it was on, it really wasn't that uncomfortable. Its inside had the softness of my favorite pair of workout pants. What was this thing lined with?

"On the box," Vendya demanded.

I grasped the skirt of the dress, and climbed onto the little pedestal. Vendya fluffed the skirt around my legs before moving to the back to close the fabric-covered buttons I'd spotted when she'd pulled it from the bag. Since our mirror was behind me, and I didn't dare mess with Vendya's process, I slid my fingers along my waist until I located the dress's pockets. I slipped my hands inside, and was pleasantly surprised to discover they were deep—and lined with the same material as whatever was on the underside of the dress. Even the boning in the bodice wasn't overly confining. It really was remarkably comfy.

You know, for a ballgown.

"*Perfekt*," Vendya praised. "And now, for the final piece."

She crossed to the garment bag and opened a zippered pouch at the top. She withdrew a tiara that glittered with blue and yellow jewels set into the shape of flowers—flowers that perfectly matched the embroidery on my dress.

"Whoa." I exhaled. "That's really cool."

"Put it on." She handed me the tiara, and I slipped it onto my head.

"How does it look?" I asked.

"Crooked."

"Well, I've never put one of these things on before, so—"

"Come." Vendya motioned for me to bend. She adjusted the tiara, and when I stood she apprised me with a self-satisfied smirk. "*Ja*. This is the dress. It will do."

"Can I look?" I asked.

Vendya twirled her fingers in a circle, which I took as permission. With a deep breath, I turned atop the box, studied the stranger staring at me from the mirror, and gasped.

"No. Freaking. Way." Elin's hushed whisper echoed my thoughts.

"It's *gorgeous*," Finna squealed.

"Seriously." Elin moved to stand beside me. My gaze shifted from my muted ivory gown to the barely pink one she wore. It also had a floral pattern, but instead of pastel blue and yellow, her flowers were a geometric tapestry of silver and fuchsia. It was modern and artsy, and so very Elin. Maybe Vendya had planned it for her all along.

My gaze returned to the clouds of fabric surrounding my hips. "This is for a dinner? It looks like a wedding dress."

Elin's lips curved. "Something you're not telling us?"

"Shut up!" I slugged her in the arm. "You look amazing, by the way."

"I do." Elin shrugged. "Guess I was off about the pink."

"I am never wrong," Vendya declared.

She definitely worked with my grandmother.

"It's a beautiful dress, Aura," Finna said. She'd changed into leggings and a tank top that hit mid-thigh—typical off-duty wear for her. "But it's so . . . fancy."

"It is for a state dinner." Vendya arched one perfectly groomed brow. "One must always appear at one's best."

"But it's cream," I pointed out. "And I'm not the most, uh, graceful eater."

"I am certain you will manage." Vendya crossed to her bag, withdrew a pin-covered pad, and strapped it to her wrist. When she returned to my side, she waved my friends away and began pinning my hem to what she must have decided was its ideal length. The process took about fifteen minutes, during which Elin twirled experimentally in her pink ensemble, and Finna filled me in on her and Jande's *Elementär* exam. When she was done, Vendya helped me step out of the dress, and Elin and I swapped spots.

"This is way better than anything I could have found for the Solstice Dance," Elin said.

"I should hope so," the seamstress huffed.

"It's going to be amazing," Elin gushed. "We've got all the decorations prepared. We just have to get into the great hall the morning of and set them up."

"You've been working every night this week." Finna patted the spot next to her on her bed, and once I'd slipped into my own tank top and leggings, I climbed after her. "You must be exhausted."

"Who isn't?" Elin shrugged. "Finals here are *way* more intense than they were back on Midgard."

"Thank gods they're nearly over." I flopped onto one of Finna's downy pillows. "After tomorrow, we're home free."

"You mean after your wedding dress dinner?" Elin pinned me with a wicked smile. "You *sure* there isn't something you're not telling us?"

"Stop it!" I considered chucking a pillow at her, but I feared Vendya's wrath far more than I wanted to extract vengeance on my friend.

"But seriously." Elin leaned forward. "If that's what you wear to a dinner, what do people wear to get married around here?"

"Stand still," Vendya barked.

Elin quickly straightened.

"Crown Princess, your gown for the Solstice Dance is in the mint-colored bag." Vendya gestured to the bed. "But you need not try it on. Now that I have your current measurements, I will tailor it to those specifications."

"Um, thanks," I said. Did I not get to look at it first? Not that I especially cared, but—

"*Perfekt!* You are finished." Vendya placed a final pin in Elin's dress, and stepped away with a wave. "Now take it off."

"Aw." Elin eyed her gown with longing.

"I will return it altered tomorrow, along with Princess Aura's pieces." Vendya released the buttons on the backside of the gown and pointed for Elin to step down. "Off."

"Fine." Elin sighed. "Never thought I'd be this into something this pink."

"You and me both." I bit back my grin. "Thanks, Vendya. Do I call you when I have an event that I need an outfit for, or . . . How does this work, exactly?"

Vendya took the dress from Elin and zipped it into its garment bag. "Eunice apprises me of their majesty's schedules months in advance. I am already preparing your gown for the Fall state dinner with Nidavellir, and I have early sketches drawn for next year's coronation gown."

"What?" I coughed. "No thanks. I opted out of the whole coronation deal. When I'm eighteen, I'm supposed to just sign some paperwork or something and it's official."

Vendya pursed her lips in a near perfect copy of my grandmother's disappointment face. "That is not how things work. One does not discard thousands of years of tradition."

"One does if one's predecessor is a despot," I muttered.

"That's next year's problem," Finna chimed in. "And you may feel differently by then."

I seriously doubted it.

Vendya left shortly after that, toting multiple garment bags and a self-satisfied smile. No doubt, she was pleased with her handiwork. And I had to admit, I was kind of excited to wear the pocketed dress. But I couldn't help but be nervous about *what* I was wearing it for.

Two more days.

Between tomorrow's state dinner and Saturday's cabinet meeting, I had two days of doing things that were *extremely* outside of my comfort zone. Then it was officially summer vacation.

I was *so* ready for that break.

CHAPTER 4

"**I**S IT FALL YET?**"** Later that night, I held tight to Viggo's hand as he led me across the courtyard. We'd taken a break from our respective exam prep to enjoy a moonlit stroll around campus. It should have induced relaxation, or possibly scored me a long-awaited make-out session. But I was too drained from my day of regent lessons, finals, and dress fittings to do more than slog listlessly after my boyfriend.

The handful of students we'd passed seemed to share my exhaustion—all of Alfheim Academy was spent from exam week. But while they only had one more day until they traded their academic worries for a summer of freedom, come Monday, I'd swap my regular study schedule for How To Be A Queen 101, constant damage control, and a master class in not ripping Narrik's head off. I'd never minded hard work, and I was grateful to be in a position to make a difference. But I couldn't help feeling that no matter how hard I tried, I'd always be underprepared.

No wonder my mom had taken that gap year.

"Hey. You've got this." Viggo squeezed my hand as we rounded a corner and stepped inside the castle. "Are you set for your *Empati* final in the morning?"

"Mostly." I followed Viggo along the empty corridor that led to our dormitory. "I'm supposed to channel those light beams in my hands and demonstrate my ability to use them as both weapons and protection."

"You ready?" Viggo asked.

"For the protection component, yes. It's basically the same thing I learned to do last term with my aura—project a shield and bring someone, or in this case, something, else inside it. It's harder with the hand beams since I have to actually create those, but it's doable. The destruction part . . ."

"Not your thing, huh?" Viggo rubbed his thumb across the back of my hand. I shivered at the light wave of goose bumps traipsing up my arm.

"I don't like accessing anything that reminds me that fifty percent of my DNA is coded to destroy."

Viggo stopped inside our common room. He angled his torso so he faced me. "You're not coded to destroy, Aura."

"I'm half dark elf," I reminded him.

"Yeah, well Ondyr is *full* dark elf. And he's one of the most decent guys I've ever met." Viggo pointed to the end of the room. Ondyr was heading upstairs, entertaining a group of third-years with a story that, apparently, involved a *lot* of hand gestures. The students followed him in varying states of laughter, while Jande trailed behind gazing adoringly at his boyfriend.

"Yeah, well." I smiled. "He's a good guy."

"See?" As Viggo led me past the fireplace, I glanced at the clock on the wall. Curfew was in three minutes—we'd definitely cut this one close. "You've got nothing to worry about. Besides, you slay with swords and that killer right hook. It's all the same, right?"

"I guess." My quads burned as I climbed the stairs. "What else do you have tomorrow?"

"I've got to run the waterfall in under thirty minutes for Conditioning, and execute a sword sequence for Advanced Weaponry. Then History of Alfheim in the afternoon, and our dinner after that."

"Yikes. Full day."

"Tell me about it." We walked in silence until we hit my floor. Our steps were slower than usual as we shuffled down the hallway. Once we reached my door, Viggo tilted his head back and closed his eyes. "I think I'll sleep for a week."

I stifled my yawn. "You and me both."

Viggo slipped his arms around my waist. "What time's your *Empati* final?"

"Nine." I rested my forehead against his chest. "But I still have to read over Eunice's briefing on Vanaheim's royal family, and—"

"Hey." Viggo lifted my chin with two fingers. "I'll help you with that at lunch. Or after our History of

Alfheim final. But you're stretched too thin. Get some sleep."

"It's our first state dinner in seventeen years," I whispered. "And we could *really* use this win."

"You can only do what you can do," Viggo reminded me. "And you're no use to us in a sleep coma."

"Yeah, but—"

"Sleep." He dropped his head and pressed his lips against mine. My pulse quickened and I stood on tiptoe, lacing my fingers through the thick, black waves of his hair as I pulled him closer. He nipped lightly at my bottom lip and I sighed, sliding my other hand along the planes of his chest. He spun me out of the doorway, pinning my back to the wall and trailing his fingers along my neck. I shivered as he shifted his attention to the sensitive spot below my ear, and I dug my fingernails into the fabric of his shirt and stifled my sigh. I didn't want to flag my roommates' attention . . . or that of the prefects who lived three doors down. But I did want to stay right here, kissing Viggo Sorenssön, for absolutely ever. He was the literal picture of calm and confidence. Whether it was because he'd been raised on a dark realm, or his parents had given him a solid foundation, or because that was him, I didn't know. What I did know was that when he held me, it was impossible to do anything but enjoy being exactly where I was, for as long as his tongue was doing the swirly thing against . . .

"Mmm." I couldn't stop myself as Viggo raked my bottom lip between his teeth.

"Shh," he reminded me.

Yeah. Right.

Viggo brought his lips back to mine. He kissed me lightly before resting his forehead against my brow. "I should go."

"Or you could not go," I said hopefully. "And we could keep doing this."

He chuckled. "Much as I'd love that, I meant what I said. You need to sleep."

"For the record, I would gladly forego sleep if you'd just go back to that thing where—"

"Aura. Viggo." The voice from my left made me jump. Renwyn, one of the prefects who lived on my floor, was emerging from her room. She wore a flowery robe, fluffy slippers, and a sleep mask atop her forehead. "Lights out was five minutes ago."

"Sorry, Renwyn." Viggo released his hold on my waist and stepped away. It took everything I had not to whine.

"Yeah, sorry," I echoed. *No, I'm not.* "We were just, uh . . ."

"I know what you were doing." Renwyn sighed. "And I don't care, except that you're doing it after curfew. And I know full well you both have exams tomorrow."

"Right." I stuck out my hand. "Well, goodnight, Viggo. Thanks for the study session. It was very . . . enlightening."

Renwyn rolled her eyes. "I'm too tired for this. Go to bed."

"On it." I saluted as Renwyn stepped into her room and closed the door.

Viggo turned to me with a quirked brow. "Enlightening?"

"Well, what would you call it?"

He stepped closer, slipping his hand around my neck and cradling the back of my head. With tantalizing slowness, he tilted his face, moving until his lips pressed firmly against mine.

Stupid Renwyn.

My breath shuddered as Viggo pulled away. I took in his hooded eyes, swollen lips, and the wrinkled shirt I'd only just released from my too-tight grip. Gods, I wanted him to stay. So very much. "You're sure you have to—"

He stopped my plea with one last kiss. "Goodnight, Aura. I'll see you at breakfast."

"See you," I muttered begrudgingly. He raised my hand to his lips and kissed my fingertips. With a wink, he turned and sauntered down the hall. I permitted myself one lingering stare before I slipped into my room and closed the door with a sigh.

Morning couldn't come fast enough.

CHAPTER 5

MORNING DID COME QUICKLY. Too quickly, from the looks of the bags under my eyes and the fog addling my brain. Despite my normal aversion to coffee, I hit the bitter liquid in the dining room with a vengeance. After two cups plus a brisk walk around the courtyard, I was ready to conquer the world—or at least, my *Empati* exam.

It took me two tries, but I successfully summoned the protective beams from my hands, encasing one of the hot pink, chipmunk-like creatures our professor had placed in a containment unit on the edge of the forest. Since I'd landed one of the more active animals as my protection subject, my teacher awarded enough additional points to make up for the fact that my first attempt had produced zero hand beams—and a borderline dangerous series of heat-inducing sparks.

Maybe the coffee had been a bad idea.

The second half of my test had gone moderately

better. I'd been the first of my classmates to success-fully blow up one of the small wooden boxes placed atop a tree branch. Not only did I not break the branch—or set fire to the tree's trunk like poor Svarri did—but I managed to disintegrate my box so that only ashes were left coating the branch where it once sat. Hopefully, my clean destroy scored me high enough to advance to fourth-year *Empati* studies—or at a minimum, move beyond the meditation modules. Zen-ing out would never be my strong point, but I was definitely getting into the whole energy-warrior thing.

Having two disciplines wasn't turning out to be as awful as I'd thought.

After lunch, Viggo, Elin, Ondyr, and I filed into History of Alfheim. The guys aced their presentation on the Alfheim-Svartalfheim conflict, fleshing out Alfheim's role in perpetrating the hostilities and earning high praise from Professor Telsha. Zara and her partner, Juli, went next. Their report examined the long-term psychological, cultural, and environmental effects of the Alfheim Barrier. It was an enlightening ten minutes. Although Eunice had given me multiple briefings on the subject, Zara and Juli covered points the palace had never brought to my attention.

"I don't understand." I raised my hand. "I knew Minister Narrik forced citizens to mine minerals, and used them to power the barrier. And obviously, that would diminish supply in the affected areas. But you're saying that he also ordered entire regions to be *stripped*? Of all usable resources? That would cause near-immediate ecological collapse."

"It did." Juli fingered the end of her lavender braid. "The mines that the minister selected for stripping became completely barren. Within a month of their depletion, the surrounding ecosystems began to die."

"How is that possible?"

"The minerals that were removed provided necessary elements to the soil. Without them, life became unsustainable. And—"

"I understand the scientific part." I flushed. "What I don't get is how Narrik could issue an order with such a destructive outcome. Anyone with half a brain would know that stripping could only have one possible result. One utterly decimating, irreversible result."

Zara tilted her head. "It's not irreversible. Or, at least, it didn't used to be."

"What do you mean?"

Zara set her note cards on the table. "My parents used to work on restoration teams."

"What are those?" Viggo asked.

"Definition's in the name, man." Ondyr shook his head. He leaned over to whisper to me, "You sure you can't do better than this guy?"

Viggo punched his friend in the arm.

"Gentlemen," Professor Telsha admonished.

"Sorry, Professor," the boys said in unison.

"Restoration teams are a partnership between *Elementär* and *Empati*. They're designed to *restore*," Zara spoke pointedly to Viggo, "the balance in an ecosystem.

The *Elementär* orchestrates the elemental components necessary to facilitate a restructuring, while the *Empati* manipulates the energy to create the ideal conditions for that restructuring to occur."

Seriously?

"And that works?" I asked.

"Absolutely. Restoration teams used to play a big part in protecting Alfheim," Zara said. "It was accepted that realms whose inhabitants draw on their resources eventually experience some degree of decline. The realms that thrive are those whose residents take care to give more than they take. The teams were the givers —they replenished what was depleted. Lots of realms use them—Vanaheim and Asgard, for sure."

My spine straightened. One of my biggest problems had just been solved by my friends' homework! *Who said school wasn't useful?*

"That's it, then!" I beamed. "That's what needs to happen. We'll send a restoration team to the meadow elves to stop their fields from dying."

"It's not that easy." Zara shot Juli an uneasy look. "Restoration teams aren't operative anymore."

"What? Why?"

"Because, Princess." Juli tugged at her braid. "The protection agency was disbanded at the start of Minister Narrik's tenure. We thought you knew that."

"I did not." I racked my brain, trying to remember if Eunice had ever mentioned the teams in her briefings. *Note to self: get a full accounting of all agencies disbanded by Minister Monster.* "Let me get this straight. Narrik ordered the stripping of regions, which was basically an ecological death warrant. And then he broke up the department capable of fixing it?"

"That's why we chose this subject for our presentation," Juli explained. "We have to find a way to make this better. But without the restoration teams, we have no idea how."

My head throbbed. I'd known the realm was broken, but I had no idea things were this extreme. Or that we'd once had the means to right our wrongs . . . and *decommissioned* the agency that oversaw them.

"Thank you, Juli and Zara." Professor Telsha made a mark on her tablet. "That was a highly informative presentation. You've given us lots to think about, and I appreciate your being so proactive in looking for alternate solutions to these long-term issues. Next, we have Elin and Aura. Ladies, whenever you're ready."

Crêpes. I'd been so focused on the debacle that was Narrik's legacy, I'd nearly forgotten it was our turn. With a nervous sigh, I grabbed my note cards and followed Elin to the front of the class. Viggo shot me a thumbs-up, while Ondyr pulled a goofy face. I shook my head and cleared my throat.

"Okay." I drew a breath. "Our presentation is on the differences between the current and previous monarchies, how they succeeded and fell short in serving the purpose of Alfheim, and how we can learn from each moving forward in a new era of Alfheim's history."

I nodded at Elin, who grasped her note cards in white-knuckled fingers. Our performance today would determine a huge chunk of our grade. Very little unnerved my best friend, but apparently failure by oral report was Elin's Achilles' heel.

"At the birth of the cosmos, Alfheim was created," Elin began. "Its purpose was to instill love and light throughout the nine realms, holding balance against those laced in darkness, and keeping our worlds from falling under their purview. Over time, our population grew and it became necessary to develop a system of governance. The Norns selected Alfheim's original ruler, Queen Osewyn, and her descendants went on to form the ruling family that has governed Alfheim through millennia, right down to our two most recent monarchies—that of Queen Helena and King Leon, and their daughter, Queen Constance."

"As time went on and populations increased, more light was needed to sustain the nine realms." I glanced at my note cards. "The Alfheim Tree was created as a transportation system. Alfheimians channeled our energy through its branches, each of which connected to a different realm—Asgard, Vanaheim, Midgard, Nidavellir, Muspelheim, Jotunheim, Svartalfheim, and Helheim."

"King Leon and Queen Helena made distribution of light a priority during their reign," Elin chimed in. "Their advisors foresaw a period of increased darkness, accompanied by an unlikely alliance between a government official and a member of a dark realm. Periodically throughout Alfheim's history, officials have been lured from the light by the promise of wealth or power.

This instance was no different, and once the perpetrator was apprehended, Leon and Helena vowed to prevent recurrences by giving more power to their constituents—most specifically, their youths. The co-regents established Alfheim Academy as a training ground in which the next generation could develop new systems to fulfill our purpose. Its presence provided its students with a sense of ownership over the well-being of the realm. *Empati* were taught to evaluate intentions so potential problems could be headed off early. *Elementär* learned to cultivate crystals to enhance, block, and channel energies. And of course, *Musa* were trained to inspire the masses."

I bit back my smile. "Queen Helena and King Leon personally oversaw the development of disciplines, curriculum, and structure still in place at the academy today. They believed that education was the single most important factor in not only creating a sense of community and purpose, but in shaping the future of their realm. Through working together for a common goal, Alfheimians would be better positioned to both achieve that goal, and improve the quality of life for citizens of *all* the realms. Their legacy was to foster education, and inspire forward-thinking youth to lead the realm to a more progressive future."

I glanced at Professor Telsha. Her approving nod eased the knot in my stomach. *So far, so good.*

"After her parents' deaths, Queen Constance ruled as they had," Elin said. "She prioritized developments in the arts, believing this to be a means to inspire everyone. And as darkness festered in those realms prone to turmoil, she increased the academy's focus on the *Verge* department, creating stronger warriors for the day when their service would be most needed."

Elin glanced at me, and Viggo nodded encouragingly. He knew what was coming—he'd listened to our rehearsal twice over the weekend. Because, boyfriends. But that didn't make this any easier to say in front of my entire class.

Breathe, Aura. It's not like they don't already know what happened.

I pulled back my shoulders, straightened my spine, and dove into my grandmother's epic failures.

"However," I began, "where Leon and Helena ruled with love, Queen Constance was guided by fear. During the early days of her rule, a faction called the *Kongelig* gained prominent roles within her cabinet. The *Kongelig* prioritized purity of bloodlines, physical and mental strength, and a willingness to fall in line for what they deemed to be the greater good. Their values were so disparate from the original purpose of Alfheim that a second faction, the *Opprør*, rose to oppose them. This party valued light, love, creativity, and inclusion. Their numbers quickly grew to outnumber the *Kongelig*, but without the regent's support, they remained the political minority. Last fall, their leaders disappeared—they have yet to return. Today, *Kongelig* figurehead, Fyrs Narrik, exercises an unhealthy level of control over the realm. Despite his continued efforts to convert Alfheim to a military state, and although the

Opprør leadership have been missing for nearly a year, we hope they will one day return and help restore Alfheim to the world it was under Queen Helena and King Leon—one filled with light, hope, and the continued reach for a better tomorrow through education, sharing of resources, and artistic inspiration."

Elin picked up where I'd left off. "While Alfheim's future remains uncertain, once the *Opprør* are restored, and proper leadership of Alfheim is sustained, it will once again be possible for peace to govern our realm. Thank you."

"Well said, ladies." Professor Telsha nodded in approval. "Take your seats—I'd like to go into a bit more detail about the missing *Opprør* leadership as a class."

Elin scurried to her chair, and I followed with a heavy exhale. We'd done it—another final exam was behind us, and our professor hadn't looked disappointed at our effort. Hopefully we'd ace History of Alfheim, and move on to whatever awaited us as fourth-years with stellar grades.

Or at least passing ones.

"Good job, *Glitre*." Viggo offered as I took my seat in front of him.

"You too," I whispered back.

Ondyr reached over to give me a high five. "Nice work, cousin."

"What am I, chopped lutefisk?" Elin raised a pointed brow.

"You did okay," Ondyr drawled.

Elin rolled her eyes at him. "You're on my list, buddy."

"When aren't I?" Ondyr retorted.

"The *Opprør* senators have been missing for quite some time." Professor Telsha's statement pulled my attention to the front of the room. "This is significant in terms of our course, because a hostility of this scope is unprecedented. Never, in the History of Alfheim, have the leading members of a political party been taken hostage without a subsequent demand."

"Meaning?" Ondyr asked.

"There have been takeovers before," Professor Telsha explained. "Threats issued between opposing parties over the years. During the times Elin and Aura mentioned, when an official accepted a bribe from a dark realm, there were even periods in which party leaders were held under duress. But in each of those cases, a demand was issued—whether monetary, or one designed to coerce a favorable vote—the abducting party's goal was always made clear. But here, we have a situation where the *Opprør* leadership disappeared on the eve of an important vote. It seems obvious that their opponents wanted to influence the outcome of that vote. And yet the *Kongelig* have issued no demand, and in fact deny all knowledge of the *Opprør's* disappearance."

"They're obviously lying," a girl in the back chimed in. "They're the ones who benefited most from the senators' absence—the admissions policies were changed so only full-blooded students could come to the academy. My sister didn't get a spot for next year."

I stared at my cuticles. Constance and I were doing everything we could to reverse that policy. But the way the laws were set up, we needed either her cabinet or the senate to support us. And since both were almost exclusively *Kongelig,* we'd hit an impasse.

"If the *Kongelig* didn't take them, then who did?" asked a boy in the front.

"Can you think of anyone else who stands to benefit from their disappearance?" Professor Telsha asked.

Viggo raised his hand. "What about Narrik?"

I tilted my head. "The *Kongelig* figurehead. Isn't that the same thing?"

"Yes," Elin muttered.

But Viggo lifted his shoulders. "We're still new here. We don't know where he came from, or who he was before he got the minister job. Could he be working independently, or is he just a cog in his party's machine?"

We all turned expectantly toward the front of the classroom.

"That's an astute question." Professor Telsha pursed her lips. "I admit, I'm not familiar with Minister Narrik's history. He declines interviews, and reveals nothing publicly. I only know that he rose to power roughly seventeen years ago, and has remained a fixture in Queen Constance's cabinet ever since."

"He's been a staunch advocate for the barrier, and admissions limitations based on bloodline since we got here," Elin offered. "So, I assume he was born here to full-blooded parents."

"Or he opened a portal from Helheim and crawled in when nobody was looking." The girl in the back snickered.

I shook my head. "Narrik's not the issue. Recovering those missing senators is."

"Exactly." Ondyr leaned forward. "But how do you find someone nobody admits to abducting?"

"Search teams have canvassed the realm, but nothing's come of it." I sighed. "Without any leads, it's been impossible to make headway."

"The loss of the *Opprør* is significant in the story of Alfheim, not only because their disappearance has shifted the political landscape, but because it marks the first time a party has fallen with no known perpetrator." Professor Telsha folded her hands together. "They simply disappeared."

My head throbbed anew, and I pressed my hands to my temples. I wasn't doing enough. Not for the missing leaders, not for the realm's ecosystems, and not for the citizens who'd depended on me to be their voice. I didn't know how I was going to fit in more than I already was, but I was painfully aware that I had to do better.

A lot of lives depended on it.

CHAPTER 6

THAT NIGHT, I STOOD behind the double doors that led to the castle's grand staircase. Vendya's ivory gown hung off my shoulders, its cinched waist flaring in layers of tulle that flowed all the way to the floor. I'd just reached to check that the flowered blue-and-yellow crown was still in place when a quiet chuckle drew my focus to the right.

"You're not going to lose it," Viggo assured me. "That dress lady sewed it on, right?"

"The seamstress pinned it," I corrected. "And still. This thing's pretty much priceless. Some Asgardian gave it to my great-grandmother. I have no idea why they're letting me wear it."

"Hey. You've got this." It had become his signature line. "Now, go out there and get in the game."

"You sound like Signy." I let Viggo hook my hand around his elbow. "But I'm pretty sure I'm going to trip on the stairs. So, look out for that."

"I won't let you," Viggo promised. And I didn't doubt his words.

"Announcing Her Royal Highness, Crown Princess Aura of Alfheim."

My heartrate spiked at the declaration from beyond the closed doors.

"We're on," Viggo said calmly. In his navy suit and silver sash, he looked as if he could have been straight out of a fairy tale. Vendya had designed his jacket to fit around his wings, and they fluttered easily behind him as he led me toward the double doors.

When they opened, I kept my hand firmly on Viggo's forearm and took small steps across the hardwood floor. My breath hitched as I caught the seemingly infinite number of faces staring from the bottom of the staircase. The royal ballroom was filled with diplomats, some I recognized, some I could only assume were visiting from Vanaheim. I spotted Minister Narrik glaring from the back corner, surrounded by his gaggle of goons. I shifted my gaze to the front of the room, where considerably friendlier faces smiled at me.

Signy and Larkin beamed from their positions near the pillars, while two of the remaining *Opprør* aides offered supportive nods. At the foot of the stairs, my grandmother wore her typically tight-lipped expression, while Eunice's face was arranged in a thin smile. Behind them stood the members of Vanaheim's royal family—an unnaturally attractive, and exceedingly tall, man and woman, and a girl who looked to be just a few years older than me. They were dressed all in white, and I hoped I hadn't committed a *faux pas* by dressing in what appeared to be their signature color. Though Vendya would have done extensive research to avoid embarrassing the crown.

I hope.

My ankles wobbled as I descended the first stair, and Viggo surreptitiously placed his other hand atop mine. With a gentle squeeze, he guided me the rest of the way until we stood firmly on the solid ground of the ballroom floor.

Step one down. Now to charm the Vanaheimians.

"Crown Princess Aura." A man to my right nodded. He extended his hand to the tall trio. "May I present their majesties, King Hakon and Queen Silvie of Vanaheim. And the crown princess, Idris."

"Your majesties." I released my grip on Viggo and executed the deep curtsy Eunice had drilled into me. I bent my knees until they nearly touched the ground while maintaining a ramrod-straight spine. After a two-second pause, I slowly rose again. Formal greetings were customary between royal families, though as co-regent I bowed to no-one on Alfheim . . . not even Constance.

"Crown Princess." King Hakon bowed at the waist, and his wife and daughter mirrored my curtsy. "It is a pleasure to make your acquaintance."

"May I present my escort, Viggo Sorenssön, of

Alfheim." I gestured to my boyfriend. When he bowed, his wings shimmered beneath the lights of the chandeliers.

"It's lovely to meet you," King Hakon said as Viggo rose. "I understand you were a tremendous asset to your realm during the recent dark elf attack."

"That's very kind," Viggo said. "Though to be frank, I was knocked out for a good portion of it. Aura had to shield the both of us."

"I heard about that." Princess Idris's violet eyes twinkled. "I can't believe your family allows you to fight. Mine would lock me away in a tower if I'd let them."

"You are extremely precious to us." Queen Silvie lifted her chin.

"I'm sure Aura is precious to her family," Idris pointed out.

To Signy, sure. To Constance . . . I stifled my snort.

"Precious might be a strong word," I said diplomatically. "How much do you know about my family history?"

"Just a bit," Idris admitted. "Your protocol advisor sent ours a breakdown that seemed to be . . . incomplete."

"Figures." I snuck a glance at Eunice, who stared at me like I was a live grenade. No doubt if I put one foot out of place, I'd be hearing about it for weeks. "My journey has been a bit unconventional."

I shot Viggo a look out of the corner of my eye. He

quickly looped my arm around his, and smiled at Idris. "But we're more interested in hearing about *your* experience, Crown Princess. I understand you've been instrumental in bringing environmental protection to Vanaheim."

"It's been the primary mission of my administration to date," Idris said. "Is that a topic you're interested in?"

"Very much," Viggo confirmed. "And Aura even more so. We were hoping we could ask your advice on the best way to implement sustainable policies."

Idris turned to me and arched her neatly groomed brows. "You're the Crown Princess. You simply implement them."

I glanced at my grandmother, now engrossed in conversation with Idris's parents. "It's not that easy here," I admitted. "Things are . . . more complicated politically than they are on your realm. But we're determined to push things through, and your initiatives have yielded remarkable success. Would you mind sharing your process over dinner?"

"Not at all." Idris tossed her white-blond hair over one shoulder. "What happens to one realm affects us all. And it's not gone unnoticed that Alfheim's suffered over the past few years."

"That's an understatement. Our—" Eunice's disapproving glare stopped me short. "Our, uh, population will benefit greatly from your expertise, I'm sure."

"You flatter me." Idris placed a hand on my arm and leaned in closer. "Also, I'm assuming the woman giving you the stink eye is your protocol advisor. Mine looks at me exactly the same way."

"Thank gods." I covered my grin with my fingertips. "I thought I was the only princess under constant scrutiny."

"Please. That's what being a princess *is*." Idris rolled her eyes. "Maybe after dinner we can sneak away and have a *real* conversation. I'll tell you all the ways I've disappointed Narissia over the years. Missed curfews, delinquent thank you notes, that time I accidentally lost one of Freya's prized cats on a diplomatic visit . . ."

"Freya, Asgard's Goddess of Love?" I balked. "You met her? Wait, did you say you lost her cat?"

"In my defense, I was only five." Idris chuckled. "And I didn't know he couldn't go outside. Who keeps a cat inside all of its life? No wonder he bolted the minute I opened the door!"

Laughter bubbled in my throat. Idris and I were going to get along *just fine*. For all the formality of her role, she seemed to be refreshingly grounded. *Thank gods.*

"Ladies, gentlemen, honored guests of the royal court." One of the pages stood in front of the gilded double doors that led to the formal banquet room. "Dinner is served."

The doors parted, and the sea of diplomats, senators, and aids moved seamlessly through the ballroom.

Viggo tilted his head at Idris. "After you, Crown Princess."

"Call me Idris," she said easily. "And I'd rather follow you. I have no idea where I'm going."

That made two of us.

With a shrug, I let Viggo guide us into the ballroom. Eunice pointed surreptitiously to the right, and we circled the table until we found place cards bearing our names. I was thrilled to discover I was seated on the opposite end of the table from Minister Narrik . . . though he still managed to shoot me a glare that would have frozen lava.

"Who is that man?" Idris whispered as she took her place to my right. "The one staring at you as if he'd like to personally see to your execution?"

She was a perceptive one, the crown princess of Vanaheim.

"That would be our minister of state." I held Narrik's gaze, refusing to be the first to break eye contact. Lesson number one of *Verge* training—never let them see you sweat.

"I take it he isn't a fan of yours?" Idris pressed.

"Fyrs Narrik is a bully," I said matter-of-factly. Narrik's nostrils flared. Had he actually heard me through all the chatter? *Yikes.* When a diplomat to his left offered him a sparkling beverage, he was forced to look away.

Score one, Aura.

"He's a dark one, isn't he?" Idris murmured.

"You have no idea," I said. "He's—"

"*Velkommen.*" My grandmother's terse voice interrupted what was about to be a very frank comment about Narrik's very unfavorable character. Constance was standing at her place, her glass held delicately in one hand. "It is my pleasure to see our honored guests, esteemed visitors, and of course, respected representatives of our own government."

Constance's eyes roamed from the king and queen at her right, down the table to Idris, and back around the opposite side. When she reached Narrik, her grip on her wine glass tightened enough that her knuckles turned white. One corner of his mouth quirked upward, her discomfort clearly giving him some kind of thrill. What the Helheim was his deal?

"This evening marks the first of what I hope will be many visits between our realms' governing bodies." Constance's thin lips pressed together in what I guessed was meant to be a smile. "King Hakon, Queen Silvie, it has been far too long since our families have gathered."

"Alfheim used to be a paragon of ethics and light—the standard other realms strove to reach. In recent years, your choices reflected your lack of care for not only your own well-being, but also that of the realms you have sworn to protect." Queen Silvie tilted her head. "However, since Alfheim has once again committed itself to share its light with *all*, Vanaheim is pleased to re-forge our alliance."

Whoa. What?

I'd known they were keeping us at arm's length, but

Eunice hadn't said anything about an alliance being formally un-forged. Had Vanaheim distanced itself because of the barrier? And if so, why hadn't that been covered in my briefing?

I made a mental note to grill Eunice later.

"Did you know anything about that?" Viggo leaned close to whisper in my ear.

"Nope." I shook my head. "Feel like that would have been worth a mention."

"Agreed." His voice was thick with disapproval.

"Well." Constance's thin smile tightened as she lifted her glass higher. "Let's hope this is the first of many mutually advantageous convenings. To our realms."

"To the light." Queen Silvie raised her own glass. The crystal sparkled beneath the chandeliers.

"To the light," repeated King Hakon.

Glasses lifted all around the table. "To the light," we echoed.

As I brought my drink to my mouth, I snuck a glance at Narrik. His lips were pursed and the skin around his eyes seemed unnaturally tight, almost as though he were fighting not to glare. No doubt, he found the toast abhorrent.

Good.

Constance sat, and I returned my glass to the table. Easy chatter filled the room as white-gloved waiters placed salad plates before us. When the staff had withdrawn, I picked up my fork and took a small bite. An explosion of flavors danced across my tongue.

"This is wonderful," Idris murmured approvingly. "Are these . . . citrus varietals?"

"Alfheimian specialty," I confirmed. "They grow during the first weeks of summer—since it's my first here, I've only just discovered them."

"That's right. I was told that you were raised off-realm." Idris raised her fork again, then chewed thoughtfully. "That must have been an adjustment."

"We both did." I placed my hand atop Viggo's. "When we were young, Svartalfheim attempted to eliminate our generation of leadership. Those of us who were born into key governing roles were sent to live off-realm to ensure Alfheim had someone to look out for it after . . . well, after them."

Idris followed my gaze to Constance and Narrik.

"And to answer what I'm sure you're wondering, no." Viggo chuckled. "Our generation doesn't intend to follow their policies *at all*."

"Gods, I'd hope not." Idris shuddered. "If the rumors are true, we're going to need Alfheim's light more than ever."

My hand tensed around Viggo's. "What do you mean?"

Idris's eyes shifted from left to right, but she kept a congenial smile on her face. "I'm sure you know, it is to your benefit to form relationships with *everyone* within your administration. Even those who may seem insignificant."

"Um . . ." I glanced at Viggo. Where was she going with this?

"You didn't hear this from me." Idris maintained her pleasant grin. "But it came to my attention that a few weeks ago, members of our household staff were approached by an outsider wanting access to the palace."

My brows shot to my hairline. "What?"

"Neutral face," Idris said calmly.

I quickly schooled my expression into the one I used in Professor Asling's meditation class. "What?" I asked again, this time sanguinely.

"Our staff is extremely loyal—none of them would ever betray us," Idris said through a smile. "But I'm not certain the same could be said of yours."

Her eyes darted to Narrik, and it took everything I had not to snort.

"Oh, he'd betray us every which way till Tuesday if he thought it would benefit him," I said confidently. "But I don't understand. Who came to your staff? And why did they want access to your palace?"

"I don't know. Those involved in the incidents have no recollection of who approached them, or what the individual's motives were. It appears their memories were altered by whomever contacted them."

It was a struggle to keep my emotions off my face. "Who could even do that?"

"A dark energy warrior," Viggo said quietly.

I whipped my head around to stare at him. "Like Dragen?"

"Or someone similar."

"Dragen." Idris bit her bottom lip. "Is he the dark elf who attacked Alfheim?"

"One and the same," Viggo confirmed. "But we incarcerated him months ago."

Actually, we'd trapped him in Hel's inner chamber, which seemed fitting for a guy who'd intended to suck out my soul. *Jeez.*

"Didn't you say that your staff were approached more recently than that?" I asked.

"Last month," Idris confirmed. "Narissia, my advisor, saw one of our ladies-in-waiting speaking to something that resembled a shadow. She reported it immediately, of course, but no wrongdoing was found. No Vanaheimian would ever compromise our realm. But it was most peculiar the way the woman had absolutely no recollection of being asked to do anything. In fact, she couldn't remember conversing with anyone at all."

"Definitely sounds like the work of an energy warrior." Viggo frowned. "If it wasn't Dragen, it must have been someone with his skill set."

"Do you think Svartalfheim's planning an attack on Vanaheim?" I asked quietly.

"They wouldn't succeed." Idris flicked her white-blond hair over one shoulder. "Our warriors have never allowed a breach."

"True," Viggo agreed. "And everyone knows it. Which means Vanaheim can't have been the target— you must have been a stop along the way."

Idris's eyes widened. "To where?"

"No idea." Viggo shrugged. "But if a dark warrior wanted access to your realm, even just as a stopover, it can't have been a good thing. Keep an ear to the ground, and let us know if anything else happens. I'm assuming your warriors increased security?"

"Tenfold," Idris confirmed. "The palace has been on lockdown ever since—and I'm not allowed to go anywhere without my guards."

Idris jutted her head at the broad-shouldered men standing discreetly against the wall behind us. Even beneath their jackets, their muscles appeared so massive, they looked like they could easily stop a fire giant . . . or five.

"I'm surprised your security isn't more substantial, Aura, considering the threat you faced not long ago." Idris took another bite of her salad.

"Things are pretty tight at the academy. And I do have a *Protektor*." I nodded at Signy, who was seated with Larkin a few places away. "Plus, I'm in a combat discipline, so . . ."

"Aura can defend herself. And when she can't, she has me." Viggo shrugged. "I'm a much stronger *Verge* than she is."

"You wish. I completely destroyed you in our final."

"You *barely* beat me," he corrected. "And I outperformed you in strength."

"Who's stuck with cleaning duty?" I challenged.

"Who's going down next term?" He arched his brow.

"I'm lost," Idris interjected. "What exactly are you two to each other? Is Viggo your bodyguard?"

"She should be so lucky." Viggo's laugh earned him a swift elbow to the ribcage. "Ow!"

"We've got the same job," I corrected.

"You're both the crown princess?" Idris' twinkling laughter bounced off the high ceiling.

"The *other* job," I amended. "We're both *Verge* Keys. We're supposed to protect Alfheim from large-scale threats."

"Wow." Idris sounded impressed. "Your government lets its princess protect the realm? I can't even go out to eat without Lars and Nars over there."

"Are those their real names?" I giggled.

"I have no idea. They swap out personnel every three days. My parents are afraid if someone sticks around too long, whoever bribed the staff will try to get to them, too." Idris sighed.

"Well, if you ever need a break, you're always welcome here," I offered. "The academy's clearing out for the summer, so we'll have plenty of extra space at the school. Feel free to come any time—with or without your guards."

"I may just take you up on that." Idris smiled. "In the meantime, looks as if the second course is here. Ooh, is that roasted terrista?"

I glanced at the gilded plate being swapped for my now-empty one. Sure enough, the queen's favorite meat dish had replaced my salad. Once the waitstaff had retreated, I leaned over to whisper in Viggo's ear, "We have to figure out who bribed Vanaheim."

"We'll put it on our list," he said easily.

I lifted my knife with a frown. Our litany of to-dos felt endless. But we'd earned Idris's trust, and learned we weren't the only realm whose security was being tested.

We had to figure out if Vanaheim's threat was somehow related to ours.

CHAPTER 7

AFTER DINNER, VIGGO, IDRIS, and I ditched the dancing and took our dessert to the drawing room. When the conversation turned to our respective upbringings, Idris, who'd spent the entirety of her childhood on Vanaheim, marveled at the fact that we'd been allowed to live off-realm. She was equal parts fascinated and horrified by Viggo's stories of Svartalfheim, and was so enthralled with my description of Midgard's comic book shops and movie theatres that she decided to make a trip of her own . . . as soon as she could figure out how to ditch Lars and Nars.

All things considered, the evening was a glowing success. Alfheim reestablished its relationship with Vanaheim, Idris promised to help me and Viggo learn to restore our realm—assuming the government let us do anything at all—and we'd gained a new ally. Plus,

Fyrs Narrik had gone home early, complaining of a stomach illness.

Sometimes life was just too good.

The next morning, exhaustion clouded my vision. My head pulsed as I wrenched my wings into my tank top, my equilibrium adversely affected by not nearly enough sleep and way more than enough cake. By the time Viggo knocked on my door, I was seriously regretting the fact that I hadn't turned in earlier. Diplomacy was important, sure. But I had my cabinet meeting in a few hours. And I could barely hold my head up.

"Morning, *Glitre*." Viggo called. "You awake?"

"Barely," I muttered. I yanked the door open to find my boyfriend looking perfect, as always. Inky waves of hair framed his un-exhausted face, and his wings fluttered easily behind his pristine black workout clothes. "How are you so perky?"

"Caffeine." He raised his arms, revealing a takeaway cup in each. "Left one's coffee, right one's cocoa. Pick your poison."

My hand snaked out to snatch the cocoa-bearing container. "Mmm. Sugar."

"Didn't you get enough of that last night?" Viggo arched one brow.

"This is a judgment-free zone." I turned my back and took a long drag. A river of chocolatey goodness traipsed its way down my throat, and I groaned. "Much better."

"You're the one who wanted to work out at zero-dark-thirty on the first day of summer." Viggo tilted his head to one shoulder, eliciting a crack. "If you'd rather get more sleep, I wholeheartedly support that."

"No. I need to be game ready for my two o'clock, and beating up on you really zens me out."

"Aren't I the lucky one," Viggo said drily.

"Mmm-hmm." I threw down the rest of the cocoa, and tossed the cup into the silver trash bin by my desk. "Let's go."

"Forgetting something?" Viggo eyed my still-bare feet.

"Right. Shoes." I darted to my wardrobe before quickly lacing myself into combat boots and meeting Viggo at the door. "What are you waiting for?"

"Last one to the training center has to clean the equipment."

"What? No. You lost in our final, and under *those* terms you're on cleaning duty for the both of us. Remember?"

"Mmm. Those two weeks start when school comes back. Today's fair game. And not to disappoint you, but I'm closer to the stairs than you are." Viggo's emerald eyes twinkled.

"Oh. It's on." I charged across the room, barreling past Viggo and launching myself along the hallway. Footsteps pounded close behind me, and when I reached the quad I stretched out my wings and leapt in the air. No way was I letting my boyfriend beat me. I hated cleaning even more than I hated politics. And since I'd be stuck doing the latter for the rest of the day, losing was not an option.

It never was.

At two o'clock, Signy, Larkin, Constance, and I stood in the private hallway of the senate building. At my urging, the queen had agreed to join me for my meeting. I wanted the meadow elves to know we took their grievance seriously . . . even if it had taken us forever to actually respond to them.

"You ready?" Signy brushed something off the arm of my fitted grey suit. Vendya had brought it to my dorm while I'd been kicking Viggo's butt in the training center.

"I rarely am." I shrugged. "But we'll give it our best, right?"

"Just remember, whatever the cabinet does, don't take their bait," Signy warned. "They've worked against our administration since you signed on, and they'd love nothing more than for you to lose your cool in front of our guests."

"I won't give them the pleasure." I raised my chin and pulled my shoulder blades down, in a perfect imitation of my grandmother's posture.

"That's my girl." Signy squeezed my bicep as a chime rang from the other side of the chamber's shiny, wooden door.

"All rise for the regents. The right honorable Queen

Constance and Crown Princess Aura are hereby presiding over this gathering of the senior members of our cabinet. This meeting of Alfheim's most reverent governing bodies is now called to order."

The doors parted, allowing me my first glimpse of the cabinet room. A long, wooden table hosted two flower-laden female elves on one side, and four stern-faced cabinet members on the other. I deliberately avoided their hate-filled glares, keeping my eyes on the man I could only assume was Alfheim's version of the town crier as he raised a futuristic-looking horn to his lips and blew. A twinkling scale resonated through the chamber, giving me time to admire his long, plum-colored coat with matching knee-length pants and a billowy white collar.

The meadow elves and cabinet members stood, turning to face me and the queen. I kept my gaze forward as I followed Constance along the aisle to take my seat on one of the two thrones—actual, legit thrones—that stood at the head of the table. The normal-sized chair to Constance's right must have belonged to Minister Narrik. He stood in front of it, brow furrowed and eyes narrowed into slits. I was pretty sure that if he squeezed his white-knuckled fists any tighter, he might very well crack his own bones.

Smile, Aura. It'll all be over in an hour.

I glanced behind me, soaking in Signy's reassuring glance. She and Larkin had come along for moral support, or protection—*or both*—and the two of them stood at the door, lending their benevolent presences to the sea of outright hostility. Now they each offered a slight nod. I tried to take solace in the knowledge that at least two people in the room didn't loathe me.

Or want me to disappear, too.

The four cabinet members shot me lethal looks as I trod carefully along the velvet carpet. This room full of jerks would love to see me fall flat on my face. Literally, *or* figuratively.

Not today, haters.

Constance reached her throne first, and I waited until she sat to follow suit. I didn't want to put a foot out of place.

The crier lowered his horn. "Adryos Nambryr, our minister of culture, will officially call this meeting to order."

The short, rotund woman standing in front of the chair next to Narrik's cleared her throat. As she did, she shot me a glare so intense I had no doubt that she was firmly Team Narrik. I silently thanked the gods that the academy was a closed facility—no doubt Minister Angry Face, or one of her colleagues, would have killed me in my sleep. No wonder the queen had bodyguards.

"*Velkommen,* esteemed cabinet members, senators, and . . ." Nambryr's lips curled in a sneer. ". . . regents."

I leaned over to whisper in Constance's ear, "She's not that into us, is she?"

"Shh," my grandmother admonished.

"This meeting of the senior members of the royal cabinet is hereby called to order. Remain standing for our opening convocation." Nambryr shot one last glare at the thrones before raising her hands to the sky and closing her eyes. She let loose with a song that, while unfamiliar, wasn't altogether unpleasant. It was a prayer to Frigga about blessing our realm, our minds, and the true purpose of Alfheim so she might shine in all her glory evermore.

Its altruism was rendered moot by the disgusted look Nambryr shot me as she plopped back into her seat.

Sigh.

"Now that the formalities have been taken care of, we can begin." Narrik lowered himself into his own seat. He glanced at the paper on the table in front of him. "Madame Sunflower and Madame Poppyseed, is it? It appears the two of you are displeased with your region's . . . weather?"

"Our displeasure is with the long-term effects of *your* senseless arson." One of the meadow elves narrowed her eyes.

"My, my. That's a serious accusation." Narrik's voice didn't lose its cool edge.

"It is well-known around the Meina region that you ordered the fire that ravaged the town. And because of that fire, *our* homelands have fallen into disrepair. Our fields no longer produce flora, our fauna have fled for lack of resources, and our residents have neither food to eat nor functions to perform. We cannot channel the flower spirits if all of the flowers have died."

Right.

I leaned forward. "Are you telling me that none of your crops can grow anymore? And your protein sources have migrated away from your colony?"

"That is correct, Crown Princess." The older elf, whose curly, white hair was tied in flowers, bowed her head. "We have subsisted largely on the grains we were able to store before the fire. But if things remain as they are, we'll be forced to find another home."

"So, you move," Narrik said coldly. "You'll hardly be the first to do so."

"But they shouldn't have to." I examined the paper directly in front of me. "According to this, you've lodged five separate requests for meetings—the first dating back to seven days after the fire."

"Yes." The younger elf's brown curls bounced. "The ash from Meina was so thick, we lived in perpetual night. It was weeks before we saw sunlight again, and by that time the first of our fields had gone barren."

"You had notice of this issue?" I stared Narrik down. "And you did nothing?"

"The realm had far more pressing matters." Narrik examined his cuticles.

"More pressing than the death of an ecosystem?" I blurted.

"It was one field, *Aura*," he sneered.

"One field led to an entire region. And you'll refer to me as your regent, *Narrik*."

The minister only scoffed.

I squared my shoulders to the meadow elves. "On behalf of the regency, this cabinet, and the entire government of Alfheim, I am sorry for our inaction, and for your loss. You have my deepest sympathy for the damage that's been ignored, along with my vow to do everything in my power to help right this wrong. We'll be launching a full investigation into the causes and possible remedies for restoring your region to proper health. And until that resolution is found, this government will assist with your colony's temporary relocation expenses."

The younger woman's eyes misted over. "We can't tell you what that means to us."

"Thank you, Crown Princess." The older woman reached over to clasp my hands in hers. She bowed her head low, and pressed it against my knuckles. "May you be blessed by the goddesses."

"Uh, you're welcome." I glanced at Constance, hoping she had some experience in meadow elf etiquette. But she remained impassive, her wings pressed against the stiff back of her throne.

"The *crown princess*," Narrik said the words as if they left a bad taste in his mouth, "speaks out of turn. She does not have the power to issue such demands. She is, in fact, powerless to act in any way."

The women turned to Narrik with wide eyes. "She is the regent."

Yeah. I'm the regent!

I stared at Narrik. "No. The minister of state speaks out of turn."

"Actually, *Crown Princess*, he doesn't." Nambryr's words came out on a hiss. "The senior members of this cabinet have authority over governmental spending. And at this time, we simply don't have funds to spare for relocation expenses."

"That can't be true." I turned to Constance. "A little help, here?"

My grandmother's eyes softened. As she opened her mouth to answer, Narrik gave a loud, *ahem.* Her gaze shifted to his and her eyes widened, painting her face in a look of barely contained panic.

"Constance?" I pressed.

"I'm afraid the minister is correct," she said quietly. "The cabinet must sign off on any governmental spending. If the senior members don't approve, then we're unable to assign funds to assist the meadow elves."

"You can't be serious." I narrowed my eyes at Nambryr. "You're saying the entire government of Alfheim has *nothing* to offer them?"

"At this time, our coffers are fully extended," she said smoothly. "Should our situation change, we'll be sure to add you to our *long* list of funding requests."

"But the crown princess said . . ." The younger woman looked at me imploringly.

"The crown princess is new," Narrik said slowly. "She has no idea what she's doing."

Rage boiled in my gut, but I stamped it down. Narrik was trying to bait me—we'd all known he would. I leaned forward and spoke directly to the women. "If these cabinet members won't assist you with funding, I'm confident they will want to take steps to restore your home as soon as possible. In the past, restoration teams worked to resolve the exact issues you're having with your region. If we reinstate them, our scientists should be able to get to the bottom of—"

"You have no authority to order a reinstatement of anything. Nor do you have the power to request a scientific inquiry, *Crown Princess*," Narrik jeered. "Government scientists are paid by this cabinet. And as we've established, the regent has no control over how we allocate our funding."

The rage bubbled hotter, my nostrils flaring as I struggled to contain it. "You've got to be kidding me."

"I never 'kid,'" Narrik said coolly. "Now, if we have no other pressing matters, this cabinet is *extremely* busy."

"You have no other business this afternoon," I pressed. "And you break for your summer recess on Monday. Surely you can spare the effort to help these women find a way to save their colony."

"Our hands are simply . . . tied." Narrik lifted his shoulders. "This meeting is hereby adjourned. Good day, ladies. Regents, a word if you please."

I *so* did not please. But I rose as the meadow elves were being escorted from the room.

As they left, I shot them an apologetic look. "I'm so sorry," I said quietly.

"You did your best." The older woman sighed. "Which is more than I expected."

My heart sank as the door closed behind them.

When I was confident they could no longer hear me, I loosened the reins on my anger.

"What the Helheim is your problem?" My hands balled into fists. "They came to us for help with a nightmare *you* created. And you let them leave with nothing?"

"Like I said." Narrik lifted his palms. "My hands are tied."

"That's a lie, and you know it. How could you turn them away?"

"I can do whatever I choose. I'm the minister of state." Narrik picked an invisible piece of lint off his sleeve. "Whereas you? Well, you have no power here. You can talk, and push, and demand all you want. But at the end of the day, you're nothing more than a figurehead. You lack any authority to do anything, ever. And so long as I'm in office, I'll ensure you stay as helpless as you are at this exact moment."

I ground my teeth together. "Then maybe you should be relieved of your duties."

A low chuckle rumbled from Narrik's chest. "I'd like to see you try."

My eyes narrowed, and I mentally girded myself for a fight. But Signy's gentle cough from the door forced me from my fury. Losing my cool would only play into Narrik's hand. And I wasn't about to give him what he wanted.

"Constance, let's go." I stood, and the town crier scrambled for his horn. Gentle tinkling filled the room, and he loudly dismissed the meeting.

When Constance, Signy, Larkin, and I were back in the private hallway, I whirled on my grandmother.

"Why didn't you support me before they threw me under the bus?" I asked.

"Because the cabinet was correct—our role *is* limited. Besides that, I didn't speak against you," Constance said. "That was my consent."

"How is doing nothing consent?" I threw a look at Signy. She and Larkin stepped closer.

"The regent's role in these proceedings is nominal. We're meant only to voice our opinion in the event we disagree with an officially proposed policy." Constance sighed. "I thought Eunice would have apprised you of this."

"She did." I spoke through gritted teeth. "But *I* thought, given the severity of repercussions, you'd have seen fit to speak the Helheim up."

"Aura." Constance stood abruptly. "You'll not talk to your queen with such language."

"You're my equal, in case you forgot." I leaned forward. "And it would have been nice if you'd had my back."

"Okay, ladies." Signy stepped between us. "I think some space is in order. Larkin, will you escort the queen to her senatorial chambers? Aura, come with me."

"Fine." I pinned Constance with a lingering glower before storming after my aunt. Signy led me through the side exit, down the stairs, and onto the lawn that ran alongside the gardens. This side of the legislative building was shielded from the senator and cabinet members' offices, affording me a break from prying eyes and disapproving looks.

Signy hooked her arm through mine, and guided me to a stone bench beneath an arch of roses. We sat in silence, staring at the thin layer of pink clouds shifting across the pale blue sky. The sun wouldn't set for another few hours, but summer evenings in Alfheim were proving even more spectacular than I'd imagined.

Too bad I was too angry to appreciate this one.

"This sucks, Signy. Those women did everything right—they asked for assistance *before* their situation escalated, then continued to ask until they finally got a meeting. We have more than enough funds, and ample *Empati* and *Elementär* who could restore the region." I pounded my fist against my thigh. "The cabinet didn't even care!"

"You were never going to win this one," Signy said calmly. "But you did well. You've set the groundwork for the next stage of your reign."

"What are you talking about?"

"You've proven yourself capable of hearing your constituents, addressing their concerns, and identifying a resolution. You've also proven that the existing administration doesn't have the long-term health of the realm in mind."

"Yeah, but what good does that do me?" My shoulders slumped. "We're exactly where we were before I was co-regent."

"For now." Signy squeezed my fist. "But I'm sure you know what you have to do?"

"Overthrow the entire existing government?"

"Return the voices of governmental reason," she corrected. "You need to track down the missing *Opprør*."

"We've had teams on that for months." I shook my head. "Those senators are gone, Signy."

"That's what their abductors want you to believe." Signy lowered her head and spoke softly. "But Larkin and I got word that one of the *Protektor* teams picked up a distress signal. They couldn't isolate the location before it disappeared, but it came from the *Opprør* leader's communicator. They're still out there. We just have to find them."

My breath caught. "How?"

"I don't know." Signy studied the clouds. "But your friends managed track an untraceable item before. I have every confidence you can do it again."

"Another task force?"

Signy smiled. "Tell me how I can help."

Resolve filled my gut. Exams were over, I'd made an ally of Princess Idris, and today's horrific meeting was behind me. Now, all of my energy could go to recovering our missing leaders. And once they were back, and their voting rights restored, maybe we'd actually be able to get things done. The right way.

It was time to get to work. *Again.*

"AURA. IT'S SIX IN the morning." Viggo's sleep-lined face filled my data pad. He ran a hand through his tousled waves, before squinting at the screen through puffy eyes. "What is so important that you're calling before the sun's up?"

"The sun came up forty minutes ago," I countered. "And I waited until six. So, you're welcome."

"Is something wrong?" Viggo yawned.

"Everything's wrong. Alfheim's being controlled by a monster, the only people who can help us are missing, and the cabinet basically told me I'd never get anything through them so I might as well go to Helheim. How hard were you sleeping?"

"We knew all that last night." Viggo's morning voice was huskier than usual. *Yum.* "We were together until curfew talking about the list of governmental failures."

"And we agreed to implement an action plan in the morning. It's morning."

"It's *six* in the morning," he said again.

"Could have called you at five," I pointed out.

"What's going on?" Ondyr's voice chimed in through the data pad.

"Aura's awake." Viggo groaned. "And now, so am I."

"We have work to do," I said.

"Stop talking so loud." Elin mumbled from the bed next to mine, where she'd shoved a pillow on top of her head.

"This affects you too, lazy. And Finna, you should—"

"I know. I'm awake." Finna sounded resigned. "Though I do want to point out, it's Sunday. Also, this is the second day of summer vacation."

"Which means we have limited time before our schedules lock down again and we have to focus on classes and homework and training. This is our only window to search for the missing leaders ourselves. Do you want to waste that time sleeping?"

"Do you really want me to answer that?" Elin grumbled. But she flung her pillow to the floor, and rolled onto her back. "Gods, it's bright. Who forgot to close the drapes?"

"I opened them an hour ago." I propped my data pad against the pillow on my already made bed, and crossed to my desk. "I also went to the great hall and snagged muffins, tea, and hot chocolate."

Elin sat. "Hot chocolate?"

"The first meeting of the *Opprør* recovery task force

begins now," I declared. "Viggo, you'd better get over here or Elin will eat all the good stuff."

"Fine." Viggo sighed. "You want me to bring Ondyr with me?"

"No," Ondyr called.

"Yep," I said. "And I'll message Zara and Wynter. Ondyr, you want to call Jande?"

"Not if I want to live. He's not exactly a fan of mornings."

"None of us are," Elin muttered.

"Guys. Future of the realm," I said.

"Right. I'll call Jande," Viggo said. "We'll be in your room in fifteen."

"See you then." The data pad blinked dark, and I poured two cups of hot chocolate.

Elin rubbed her eyes as I handed hers over. "You're dressed already?"

"I wasn't going to go to the dining hall in my pajamas." I shrugged. "Now get ready. We have a lot to do."

With a sigh, Elin swung her legs over the edge of her bed. She sipped her drink as she shuffled to the bathroom. Once she was inside, I handed the second cup to Finna.

"We're going to be okay. Right?" My teeth worried my bottom lip.

"We'll keep doing everything we can," she assured me. "It's all we can do."

"I know." I dropped into the desk chair. "I just . . . after yesterday I feel so helpless."

"Don't." Finna shook her head. "We're going to set

this right. It may take time, and a *lot* of setbacks, but we'll figure it out."

I reached over to clasp her hand. "Thanks, Finna."

"Of course." She set her beverage on her nightstand. "Now let me get ready before your gorgeous boyfriend sees me with bed hair."

Right.

Twenty minutes later, our normally spacious dorm room felt uncharacteristically cramped. Zara sat on my bed beside Wynter, the *Bridger* who'd used her unconventional gifts to introduce me to my deceased dad a few months back. . . and later, to help our team defeat my evil uncle Dragen. Viggo and Ondyr claimed desk chairs, and Finna had moved over to Elin's side of the room . . . since Jande was sprawled out across Finna's bed.

"Comfy?" Finna raised a brow at her friend.

"As I can be, after *somebody* woke me up this early on the first day of summer vacation. Not that it isn't for a worthy cause," Jande added, as I opened my mouth to berate him. "I'm answering the question honestly."

Fair.

"Let's get started then." I paced in front of one of the big, open windows. The cheerful trill of songbirds floated across the sill. "As you guys know, I couldn't get the cabinet to help the meadow elves—or their habitat. Narrik slammed my suggestions before they ever had a chance."

"I really hate that guy," Elin grumbled.

"You and me both," I agreed.

"I can't believe they ever did away with the restoration teams." Zara frowned. "They'd have been a slam dunk to fix that problem. It's a real shame Minister Narrik shut their department down."

Elin turned to me. "You're the diplomat—how do you get a department reinstated?"

"It would have to go through a resolution process," I said. "You'd need a well-drafted proposal, a formal submission before the senate, and two-thirds approval by the voting bodies."

"The regent's vote counts for one-third, right?" Elin asked.

"Correct. With the cabinet and the senate constituting the other two."

"And we haven't tried this . . . why?" Elin pressed.

"Because there's zero chance of anyone but me and Constance passing that proposal." I shrugged. "We'd be wasting our time. Besides, I'm not familiar enough with the former practices—or the whole *Elementär* crystal-regrowing thing—to speak in front of the senate without embarrassing myself."

"Maybe now, but . . ." Elin glanced at Finna. My science-geek roommate nodded.

"We'll draft it," Finna said. "It may take us a while, but we'll put together something technical—in words you can totally explain," she added before I could object. "You can present it at the next senate session."

"Are you sure?" I glanced between Elin and Finna.

"We have Jande." Finna shrugged. "He's top of our

class in crystals, and I'm sure he'll need something to do now that classes are out."

"I'd *intended* to sleep." Jande didn't move his arm from over his eyes. "But if you all need my big brain so badly, who am I to say no?"

That was Jande. Big brain, bigger ego.

"Well, thanks." I grinned. "Okay, so about my meeting yesterday. After I'd finished venting to Signy about the cabinet's total refusal to do *anything* helpful *ever*, she pointed out that we're not going to get squat done without the *Opprør*. And until their leaders are returned, we've got zero chance of making the changes Alfheim needs to survive. So, we're going to track them."

"Um." Jande raised his hand. "Haven't official teams been on that for months?"

"Yes," I said. "Clearly, they lack our motivation."

"Not to be the group downer," Jande continued. "But what do you think we're going to be able to do that they can't? They have actual warriors on this —*Protektors*, and guards, the whole deal."

"The same *Protektors* and guards who tried to find the crystal last fall and failed. We pulled that off, didn't we?" I set my hand on my hip. "We're going to do this too."

"I like your confidence, *Glitre*." Viggo popped a piece of muffin in his mouth. "So, what's the plan?"

"I'm not entirely sure," I admitted. "But we've got a pretty diverse collection of strengths here, and if we play to them, we'll figure it out. We have to."

"Seriously," Zara chimed in. "We're the ones who are most affected by all of this. It's our school losing students who don't fit their mold, and our realm that's being destroyed. Those senators will be long dead by the time things are completely shot, and we'll be stuck living in some dystopian nightmare."

"Been there, done that," Ondyr muttered. "Z, I'll run a ground search with you if you're up for it."

"Done." Zara nodded at me. "Put us down for a search team. Whatever region you think might generate a lead."

"Thanks." I grabbed my data pad and made a note.

"I'll cover things from the Cloak," Wynter referenced the hidden void through which her department bridged communications between the living and the dead. "Most of the *Bridger* students are going home for break, so it'll be easy for me to monitor the incoming messages and to put out feelers about what we're looking for. I'll pass anything I hear to whoever's running operations from the ground."

"I'd propose Finna and Jande do ground ops." I glanced at my friends. "Since you're not combat trained, I don't want to put you in the field unless we have to. And besides, you have access to crystals that do things we can't."

"What are you thinking?" Finna tilted her head.

"Remember that stone that broke Bob's curse? Ungargoyled him?"

"Diamond aventurine. What about it?" Jande asked.

"Well, since nobody's been able to track the missing

Opprør, I'm wondering if there's some kind of protection around them. Like an energetic blocker that's keeping us from seeing them. Or sensing them. Or whatever the trackers have tried so far." I tapped my finger to my jaw. "There has to be a reason they can't be found."

"And maybe there's a crystal that can break whatever block's in place." Finna's eyes sparkled. "We're on it. We'll handle communications between the teams, identify potential blocks, and procure the crystal remedies."

"Nice." Jande nodded in agreement.

"I'm assuming we'll be taking a search area." Viggo arched a brow at me.

"We'll take the farthest regions, since we've got the wings." I made another note on my pad. "All this is good."

"What can I do?" Elin asked.

I turned to face her. "Will you take ground ops with Finna and Jande, but also work with Signy? She and Larkin have access to information we don't, since they're *Protektors.* They may be able to pinpoint something in their briefings or interactions with the warriors that's just suspicious enough to give us a lead."

"On it." Elin took another hit of her cocoa. "The *Kongelig* are stupid. I'm sure they've slipped up somewhere."

"Let's hope so." I set my data pad on the desk. "If we don't get those senators back, things are going to keep getting worse."

"We'll find them," Viggo vowed. "We've done the impossible before, with fewer members. Between the eight of us, we're a force to be reckoned with."

"A faerie force." Jande waggled his brows at Viggo's wings.

Oh, honestly.

"So, it's settled," I said. "We'll take off tomorrow, and—"

"Um . . ." Jande raised his hand again. "Did you forget about the Solstice Dance?"

"Viggo and I are out." I shook my head. "If we're tackling the remote regions, it'll take us a while to get there. I don't want to waste any time."

"Dancing's not a waste of time," Jande muttered.

Ondyr and Zara exchanged a nod.

"Zara and I are out, too," Ondyr chimed in. "I don't want to go back to living in a dystopia. Svartalfheim was bad enough."

"Fine. We'll work through the dance." Jande sat to point his finger at me. "But you owe me, Aura Nilssen. When you're queen, you'd better throw the biggest coronation ball this realm's ever seen. And you'd better have that seamstress of yours make me an outfit that's *to die for.*"

"I don't want a—" I clamped my lips together as Ondyr shot me a death glare.

"I won't hear the end of it," he muttered.

Seriously?

"Oh . . . fine. Jande, I'll throw you a ball. A small one," I added as his face lit up.

"You will not regret it," he trilled.

I already am.

I sighed. "I'll prepare an operations breakdown and have copies ready for everyone by morning. Meet here tomorrow at eight a.m., and we'll go over any questions before the ground teams take off."

"Let me and Elin prepare that breakdown." Finna placed a hand on my arm. "You have enough on your plate."

"But you don't know all of the—"

"I'll help them," Viggo said. "You're doing that weird twitching thing with your jaw again that usually means you've got massive sleep deprivation. And if I'm traveling with you for an indeterminate period, I'd rather you *not* be off your rocker."

I crossed my arms. "What are you saying?"

"I'm saying you need to take a nap," Viggo said. "The three of us will get this drafted while you sleep, and when it's done, we can all go somewhere *relaxing*. Like the river."

"Or the waterfall." Ondyr pushed himself off the chair and stretched. "If we only get one day of summer, we'd better live it up. Swimming, anyone?"

"I'm in." Zara stood. "Wynter?"

"Why not?" Wynter slid to her feet. "Meet you in the quad in an hour?"

"Good. That'll give me time to shower." Zara chuckled. "When I got Aura's '*My room, now!*' message, I figured I'd be in for it if it took my time."

"I waited until six a.m." How many times did I have to say it?

"And that's what'll make you a great queen," Viggo said. "But as a classmate . . . on the first weekend of vacation . . ."

"Get out of here." I rolled my eyes.

"Bring lots of sunscreen, Wynter. You're going to need it." Jande held his sun-kissed arm against Wynter's chalky one.

Ondyr nudged Jande forward. "You've got one day of summer vacation. Do you really want to waste it teasing the *Bridger*?"

Wynter shrugged. "He can tease me all he wants. I'll just sic a water spirit on him."

Jande froze. "You wouldn't dare."

"Try me." Wynter arched one brow. When Jande scurried from the room, she shot Ondyr a playful wink. "Feel free to use that one if you ever need to motivate him."

Ondyr laughed. "Duly noted."

"Though if you do need any, I've got enough sunscreen for the both of us." Zara followed Wynter and Ondyr out of the door. As she walked, she tugged her crimson curls into a loose ponytail. "Redhead problems."

"Is that why you're always so angry in the training ring? Sunburn-phobia?" Ondyr shot over his shoulder.

"Nope, that's because it's too easy to kick your butt," Zara fired. "I thought a guy from Svartalfheim would make a tougher training partner."

Ondyr's easy laughter echoed from the hallway.

Once the door clicked shut, I turned to Viggo, Elin, and Finna. "You guys sure you're up to writing the breakdown?"

"We'll have it done by lunchtime," Finna promised.

"Now go to sleep," Elin ordered. "And for the love of Frigga, please *never* call a six a.m. meeting again."

"The fate of the realm is *literally* in our hands," I reminded her.

"And the fate of my sanity is *literally* in yours. No more early meetings." With that, Elin shoved me toward my bed. She grabbed her data pad and waved Finna and Viggo toward the door. "Let's go, you guys. The sooner we get this written, the sooner we can go relax—for one day."

"Fate of the realm!" I called as the door clicked closed. With a rueful smile, I dropped my head onto my pillow and stared at the ceiling. Elin had my back. She always had.

Now we just had to make sure that we had Alfheim's.

CHAPTER 9

THE NEXT MORNING, MY team met in the academy's courtyard. Signy stood beside Ondyr and Zara, both of whom were bent over stretching. Elin, Finna, and Wynter scrolled through their respective data pads. And Jande was shifting contents between two packs, his tanned arms glinting in the early morning sun.

"Fine. I'll pull the amethyst, but I'm packing you malachite, whether you want it or not." Jande looked up from one of the bags. "It's a protection stone, and it *will* shatter if danger is nearby so I strongly advise that you keep it somewhere you can check to see if it's in one piece."

"We don't want any more weight than necessary," Ondyr said calmly. "And stones are—"

"Are you saying you can't carry one teensy, extra crystal?" Jande stared pointedly. "With *all* of that muscle?"

"It's not the one extra thing we're worried about," Zara countered. "That bag has, like, twenty different rocks."

"Crystals," Jande corrected. "And excuse me for caring about you."

"How about you pick your favorite five, and we'll take those?" Ondyr offered.

"Fi—are you kidding me? Do you really expect me to choose between protection and synchronicity and neutrality and grounding and rejuvenation and—"

"Five," Zara repeated. "You can do it, Jande."

"You can," Ondyr agreed.

"Oh, honestly." Jande frowned. But he turned to the bags and withdrew several crystals.

"Five for us, too." I laced my fingers through Viggo's as we crossed the grass. "Assuming you packed us crystal kits."

"Do you think I don't love you?" Jande glanced my way. "Of course I packed you kits. But since you're traveling farther than Ondyr and Zara, I'd really recommend bringing ten stones—fifteen, maybe."

"Nope. Five. Same as those guys." I nodded at the *Verge* who were stretching on the lawn. Then I raised a hand to my aunt. "Morning, Signy."

"Good morning." Her eyes twinkled. "You kids were out awfully late."

"And I'm definitely regretting it," I admitted. "No, Jande. I said *five*. I see you trying to sneak in more."

"Oh, fine." Jande shuffled shiny rocks between four gauzy bags and his pockets before settling on his choices. "Here. Take them. Don't blame me if your trips are unharmonious, unbalanced, and filled with unnecessary accidents and upheavals. My original sets were *perfekt.*"

"I'm sure they were. But flying's hard enough without the added weight." I took the offered bag, and tucked it into the shoulder pack I'd fastened across my chest. Wings made backpacks difficult, but Viggo and I had managed a workaround. "Oh, good—you guys brought the daggers from the *Verge* center. Thanks."

I bent to retrieve one of the small blades from a pile on the lawn. I slipped it into the holster on my belt, and snapped its latch closed. "I think that's it for me."

"Me too." Viggo weaponed up before slipping Jande's crystals into his own bag. "Finna, have you sent us our coordinates?"

"I just did." Finna looked over from her data pad. "Check your comms; they should be there."

I activated the watch-like device on my wrist, scrolling through until Finna's transmission appeared "We're going due north," I confirmed. "Past the meadowlands, and into . . . *kindur* country?"

"Yes," Finna confirmed. "There are plenty of caves there, and it's remote enough that it's difficult to track inhabitants. It could be an ideal place to hide something—or *someone*—you don't want found."

"A lot of someones," I said. "We're looking for around twenty senators total, right?"

"Correct." Elin pressed a button on her data pad. "Ondyr and Zara, your coordinates are coming in now.

You're going south—not as far away as the winged team, but to another location with plenty of caves. The beaches on the Tyraste Sea."

"It's sea-dragon season, so be careful near the water," Wynter warned. "The tiny ones are venomous."

"Good to know." Ondyr attached a dagger to his belt before passing one to Zara. "Anything else?"

"Yeah. There have been mudslides in the region thanks to recent erosion, so make sure you scout the entrances before going into any caves." Elin made a note. "And try to establish a secondary exit route before entering."

"Don't get poisoned by sea-dragons, and don't get buried in a cave." Zara saluted. "Sounds like a plan."

"Keep your comms on, and let us know when you've reached your destinations," Finna advised. "Ondyr and Zara should be clear the whole time, but Aura and Viggo, reception may be spotty where you're going. Just check in with us whenever you get a signal."

"Will do," Viggo confirmed.

"Wynter will be passing information from the Cloak, and anything she learns we'll relay to you," Elin reminded us. "If you run into any trouble, come home. We're already down our senators; we can't afford to lose anyone else."

"We'll be back before you know it." I said it to convince myself as much as anyone else. This was only a fact-finding mission, not an actual extraction. Even so, I couldn't ignore the butterflies jostling inside my stomach. An entire political party had disappeared.

Fyrs Narrik wanted me and Constance gone, too. And somewhere out there, a dark energy warrior was trying to make deals with our allied realms.

Was taking off really our best idea?

As she always did, Signy seemed to read my mind. She quietly crossed to stand beside me, and slipped her arm around my waist. "I wouldn't let you do this if I didn't think you could handle it. You've more than proven yourself—all of you."

"I know," I said. "And I know we'll be fine. It's just . . ."

"There's a lot riding on this," Viggo spoke up. "But we'll handle it the same way we do everything else. As a team."

"An epic team," Elin chimed in. "We kicked that Huldra's butt, didn't we? And your uncle's? Sorry, Ondyr."

"Don't be." Ondyr shook his head. "I'm one hundred percent Team Alfheim."

"We'll get the intel, and we'll use it to make sure we find our senators," Viggo vowed. "And then we can get back to focusing on what *really* matters—restoring the realm."

He said the last words at the same time Ondyr said, "Summer vacation."

The two exchanged grins.

"Everybody double check that your comms are working," Signy instructed.

"Mine's good," Elin said.

"Mine too," Finna and Wynter added.

"On," I said.

Viggo nodded, Ondyr raised his fist, and Zara gave a thumbs-up.

"All right then. Be *very* safe," Signy ordered. She turned and pulled me into a hug. "Especially you, missy. Viggo, take care of my girl."

"You know I will," he promised.

"More likely she'll be taking care of him," Elin joked. But she came over and joined in Signy's hug. "Seriously, Viggo. She gets hurt, I hurt you."

"Noted." He chuckled.

"Report back with any intel, and reconvene as soon as you can." Finna tapped her comm. "Travel safely, friends. And may the light be with you on your journey."

I squeezed Signy and Elin tightly. When I released them, I turned to Viggo with a nervous smile. "You ready?"

"Walk in the park, *Glitre*. We've got this." With a grin, he leapt into the air. He stretched his wings out and flapped until he hovered above the quad. "Let's go."

I shot Signy one last, anxious grin, before running across the grass and extending my wings. With a flap I was off, soaring high above the castle, and into the unknown.

Seven hours later, my back ached, my abs screamed,

and I was almost positive my wings were going to fall right off.

"Any chance we're almost there?" I shouted to be heard over the wind. The gusts had begun hours ago, turning what should have been an eight-hour flight into what seemed to be a never-ending one.

"My comm says we still have a way to go." Viggo glanced at his wrist. "After we clear these salt flats, there's a forest, then another forest, then the meadow-lands. *Then* we're almost there."

I rubbed at my neck. "Great."

"If you want, you can draft me," Viggo offered. "Get a break from the wind."

"Yeah, thanks. We can swap in five."

"No need. Unlike some people, I could do this all day." Viggo shot me a rakish grin.

"Please. You were literally *just* whining about how tired your—"

"I was not whining. In fact, I . . . uh-oh." Viggo glanced at his comm. "There's another storm ahead. If the winds are as strong as this says they'll be, I may need to draft you after all. You take the first rest."

He didn't have to ask me twice. Every muscle in my torso was on fire.

How did everyone else do this? Was there even anyone I could ask? Besides my grandmother, who I definitely couldn't picture doling out athletic advice, I'd only seen one or two others like us. Where were all the *älva*, anyway?

"Hey," I called as I tucked into Viggo's draft. "Your

parents had wings, right? Did they ever tell you how many of us there are?"

"I don't think there are a lot." Viggo spoke over his shoulder. "My dad said most of the *älva* scattered to remote areas to avoid detection. We have more abilities than light elves, and apparently the queen's administration was abusing *älva* for their magic."

"Shut up. We have magic?"

"You have glowing hand beams, don't you?"

Fair.

"Did your parents have magic?" I amended.

"Dad had light beams, same as you." Viggo's shoulders rose. "And Mom had dust."

"Dust?"

"Yeah. Some *älva* produce a powder that holds the resonance of their energetic gifts. It lets them share their abilities with non-magical beings. In the right hands, it's great. But if someone intent on destruction —or exclusion—gets a hold of the dust . . ."

Recognition bloomed. "That's why everyone else moved away."

Ahead of me, Viggo swerved to avoid a fresh gust. I lowered my head and followed suit. "From what my dad told me, Narrik rounded up a bunch of *älva* and locked them in some government facility. Those with abilities were put to work bolstering the barrier's security, while those with dust were forced to produce until they were depleted."

"That's terrible." I followed Viggo back to the right. "Are those facilities still operating?"

"They were allegedly shut down once the barrier was lifted," Viggo said. "But do you really think Narrik would forfeit access to that kind of power?"

"I can't believe nobody told me about this." I flapped my wings so I could pull alongside Viggo. "First thing we do when we get home is talk to Constance. We need to make sure everyone who was incarcerated is released—and that Narrik won't force them to do anything for him, ever again."

Viggo turned his head, revealing a dimple. "How did I know you were going to say that?"

Another gust knocked me off course, and I glanced below as I steadied myself. "Holy gods, what happened there?" I slowed just enough to study the ground.

Below us, a once-vibrant forest had faded to a sea of sickly grey and puce. Tree limbs crooked at unnatural angles as if they'd been frozen in place while shirking an onslaught . . . or running from a blanket of death.

"*Skit,*" Viggo swore. "I've never seen anything like it."

"That's not drought-induced."

"Definitely not." Viggo scanned the ground. "The trees would be drier—and brown, not grey. There must be some kind of contaminant in soil. But from what?"

"I don't see any streams, so there can't have been a pollutant." I craned my neck. "And the ocean's too far away for something to have washed in. I'm guessing this area got its water from rainfall. Is there acid rain in Alfheim?"

"I'm a *Verge.* We don't take science."

Right. I made a note to ask Finna what could kill an entire forest.

"Whatever it is, do you think we should turn around?" I ventured. "If it's airborne, it could affect us."

"I'm sure it could," Viggo agreed. "But our lead sent us this way, and until we're in actual danger we should—oh, *skit*. Cover your mouth. It's coming straight for us."

I snapped my head forward. My nostrils flared as I spotted the enormous, dark cloud. It raced toward us like a cluster of angry locusts. Its swarm of chalky, black residue swirled violently in an onslaught of fury. Angry hissing filled the sky, and my gut churned at the darkness resonating in the air. Any second now it would hit us, and I had zero doubt the contact would be painful—possibly excruciating. Acid rain hadn't been responsible for the decimation below. My gut told me this cloud had done the job . . . and whatever had happened to that forest was about to happen to us.

"Look out!" I flung myself into Viggo, burying my face against his chest and wrapping my arms around his head. With a breath, I tapped into the energy surrounding me and pushed it outward. The bubble encased me, and I pressed against its edges until it covered Viggo, too. White-hot burns pricked at its surface as we maneuvered through the cloud, and I ground my teeth together until we'd reached the other side.

Once we were free of the darkness, I released my

hold on Viggo and shook my wings, putting extra distance between me and the death-cloud.

"What the Helheim was that?" I blurted.

Viggo flew so we were again side by side. "No clue. But whatever it was, it didn't want us to get through."

"Which means we must be closer to what we're looking for than we thought. Come on—before another monster cloud attacks us."

"Don't have to ask me twice." Viggo flapped his wings, and we soared over the rest of the forest in silence. The wind increased again over the meadowlands, and I waved Viggo behind me, directing him into my draft.

"Take a break," I offered. "The meadows were the last landmark, and Frigga only knows what we're going to run into once we reach the caves. You'd better rest."

"I'm fine." Viggo grimaced. "I'd rather we be together if anything's coming. Besides, I'm not that tired."

Show-off.

But I didn't give him a hard time. The truth was, I appreciated not taking point now that we were this close to our mysterious destination. And as we flew over herds of wooly sheep the size of baby elephants, I couldn't help but wonder about the creatures who dedicated their lives to herding them.

If they could control animals that massive . . . what would they be able to do to us?

"**STAY BEHIND ME, AURA.**" Viggo raised one fist before landing atop a knoll. "I don't see the animal's keepers, but that doesn't mean they aren't here."

"You think the shepherds can turn invisible?" I shook my head as I landed beside him. My legs were wobbly after a full day of flying, and it took me a minute to get my bearings.

"I don't know what I think." Viggo scanned the meadow. "But I'd definitely rather they shoot at me than you. I'm better at defense than you are."

"Hey." Despite my objection, I let him stand in front of me as we both turned in a slow circle. Because, chivalry.

We had a clear view of the meadow from our knoll-top vantage point. The grass butted against a jagged mountain range, the inside of which I assumed contained the caves we'd come to search. I hoped they were animal-free. This far north, we'd anticipated finding birds and deer and a handful of small mammals —not oversized sheep . . . or the massive, curved horns that topped their heads like lethal crowns.

Death by sheep-goring was *not* how I wanted to go.

"Maybe they're wild," I said quietly. "They don't seem to be moving, and I don't see collars or bells or anything. So . . . is it possible they just live here on their own? Unsupervised?"

"Maybe," Viggo said doubtfully. "But Finna was pretty thorough. If there were wild sheep, she'd have flagged it in her—"

"Intruders!" a deep voice boomed from the sky. "Identify yourselves!"

Oh, gods.

My hand flew to my waist. I drew my dagger and bent my knees in a deep fighting lunge. Breath whooshed from my lungs as I locked eyes on a man hovering directly above me. His thick arms, lean waist, and silver wings left little doubt that he was not only an *älva,* but an extremely strong one. The broadsword he clutched in one hand suggested that he was a warrior . . . probably one sent to rid the region of threats.

Threats that currently included me and Viggo.

Gulp.

I glanced at my partner, who had his own blade drawn. We were fast, but there was no way we could take on a sword that size with our daggers. We'd have to disable our assailant first, wrestle control of the broadsword, and possibly use it on him. But we'd faced worse. And there were two of us and one of him. We could totally do this.

"Identify yourselves or leave," the man repeated. He raised his sword threateningly. "Intruders here are executed on sight. But you seem young, so I'll give you two counts before I kill you."

Since he hovered between us and the caves, there was a good chance he was protecting whatever was inside them—possibly our stolen senators. Either way, we weren't getting past him without a solid excuse . . . or an even better attack.

"It's your funeral," the man growled. "One. Two."

"Zeta formation." I spoke without moving my lips. "Now!"

I pulled my shoulders back and leapt into the air, darting to the right so I could circle our attacker and strike from behind. Out of the corner of my eye, I saw Viggo move in on the front of him. His dagger swiped at the man's calf, forcing him upward and right into my range. I drew my arm behind me as I flew forward, ready to sink my blade between his shoulders. But just before I reached him, he flung himself to his right. With a massive *oomph*, he collided with Viggo. Their bodies tumbled toward the ground, a tangle of legs and wings and blades. They landed on the grass, grappling fiercely while I tucked my arms to my sides and dove.

My heart seized when the man shoved his forearm

to Viggo's neck, pinning him in one debilitating move. My partner kicked violently, a pointless attempt to dislodge the considerably larger man now straddling his torso. Viggo's face purpled with the struggle. As he fought for air, I flew even harder.

I'd nearly reached him when the man leaned back. Shock colored his angular features as he blurted, "Viggo?"

"Yeah," Viggo grunted. He arched his spine and kicked again.

"My gods, Viggo, is that you?" The man released his choke hold.

"Who the Helheim are you?" Viggo coughed.

My feet landed hard on the grass. Pain shot from my heels to my knees, but I ignored it as I raced to Viggo's side. The man stood, bringing his hand to his neck as he paced across the grass.

"Stay away from Viggo." I challenged. I quickly scanned my boyfriend, who appeared to be breathing all right on the ground. Since our attacker posed a more immediate threat than asphyxiation, I jumped in front of Viggo and raised my dagger. "How do you know him?"

"I heard you were dead." The man paced faster. "The reports came in from Svartalfheim—they said your bones were recovered. But—"

"Wait a minute." I lowered my dagger. The man's wavy, dark hair, his emerald eyes. Even the way he moved, holding his shoulders low as if the weight of his muscles strained his long frame—he was too familiar to be a stranger. And yet, Viggo's parents were dead.

Weren't they?

The man's pacing continued. Since he didn't seem inclined to attack us again, I offered Viggo my hand. Without taking his eyes off the man, Viggo rose unsteadily to his feet. Once standing, his knuckles cracked around the hilt of his dagger.

"Who. The Helheim. Are you?" Viggo repeated.

The man finally stopped moving. His wings flickered behind him, and for the first time my eyes caught on the shimmering, glitter-like particles floating between them. They moved in tight infinity-symbols, linking the appendages together. When the man shook his head, an inky wave of hair slipped from the knot atop his head. His eyes crinkled at their wrinkle-lined corners as his lips formed a sad smile. A dimple flashed as he studied Viggo with . . . was that affection?

But they're dead. Viggo told me they're dead.

My eyes widened. The man was older, but he was without a doubt the aged version of—

"Viggo." The man exhaled. "Forgive me. It's been so many years, and I didn't think I'd ever see you again."

"Last chance." Viggo drew his dagger arm back. "Who are you?"

"Your father's brother," the man said quietly. "I'm Rafe Sorenssön."

What?

Viggo froze, his face a mask of pure shock. "You're my uncle?"

Rafe's eyes glistened, moisture filling their emerald depths. Was the guy who'd been about to kill us actually crying?

"But you fled. When the barrier went up, my dad said you'd gone . . ."

"I came here," Rafe said. "It wasn't safe for us anymore. Your father was a warrior—he was exempt from the internment orders. But when the government issued the demand that all non-military *älva* report to work on the barrier, we knew what it meant. My tribe defected immediately. We'd heard there were regions in the north that were so far removed from civilization, even the royal trackers couldn't find them. We settled in these caves, and we've lived off the land ever since."

"They never found you?" Viggo asked.

"Believe it or not, you two are the first outsiders to make it past the dead forest."

"You placed the black cloud," I offered. I held tight to my dagger as I walked to Viggo's side. "Anything else we should be aware of?"

"More traps guard alternate entrances to the meadow." Rafe studied me with unnervingly intense eyes. "But they will not harm you. Now that I know who you are, I can program them to permit you to pass."

"Gee, thanks."

Rafe tilted his head. "How did you get past the cloud? You're very young to manage a protection of that level."

"Aura's a high-level blocker," Viggo said. "My plan was to cover my mouth and hope for the best."

Rafe frowned. "The acid would have eaten through your skin by the time you took your first breath. It's a good thing your companion is wiser than you are."

"She usually is." Viggo's dimple popped.

"Well. No doubt you've traveled a far way. Let us feed you. You can tell me over dinner what it is that's brought you such a great distance from . . . where are you living now, Viggo?"

"I'm at Alfheim Academy. Aura is too. All the Keys are."

"Yes, I've not forgotten the role you were meant to play in serving our realm. Are you training to be a warrior, like your father?" Rafe asked.

"In a sense." Viggo glanced at me, and I nodded. "Aura and I are both *Verge*. We're meant to protect Alfheim."

"Aura the *Verge*. And, if I'm not mistaken, the regent as well." Rafe turned his attention to me. "I've heard whispers of you. Even a region as remote as ours is aware of the changes you have brought to our realm. Changes that have been a long time coming."

"Yeah, well." I toed the ground. "We're hoping we can make some of them stick. That's why we're here. Some of our senators were abducted, and we don't know where they are. We need to find them and bring them home. They're the ones who actually have the power to make a difference."

"We'll do all we can to help you," Rafe vowed.

"We?" The only other lifeforms in the meadow had

four legs, wool coats, and massive horns on their heads. *Right?*

Rafe held out his hand. "Come with me, Aura. Viggo, I'd like to introduce you to the rest of your family."

CHAPTER 11

"THE REST OF MY . . ." Shock coated Viggo's normally even-keeled features. We trailed behind Rafe, whose still-glittering wings fluttered in the afternoon breeze.

"Did you know about them?" I whispered as we walked.

"No. My dad told me he had a brother, but since we lived on Svartalfheim most of my life, I never met him. And my mom's parents were killed in the line of duty. They were warriors, too."

"I'm sorry," I murmured. We'd cleared the meadow, and now stood in front of the massive cliffs.

"Yeah, me too. I wish I could have met them—Mom said they were something else." Viggo shook his head.

Rafe slipped into an opening between the rocks, and motioned for us to follow him. Viggo wrapped his fingers around mine and took the lead.

The entrance to the cave was dark and narrow,

jagged rock formations stretching from the dirt a good twenty feet overhead. I kept my attention on my footing, careful not to trip over the small stones that littered the ground. I was so focused on not falling that I didn't look up until we'd made it through the entryway . . . where a vast cavern now stretched before us.

"Holy *skit*," Viggo swore.

I sucked in a breath as I stared at the massive space. It easily stretched the length of two football fields, and was filled with every conceivable arrangement for socializing. Children played games on carpeted squares framed by love seats, and adults chatted and ate around a table-lined buffet. At the far end of the space, a massive patch of grass hosted a mixed-age group playing what appeared to be a rugby game

How did all of this fit inside a *cave*?

I angled my head back and tried not to gape. The room extended a full hundred feet in height, with sconces providing up-lighting on the walls, and fairy lights strung artfully across the ceiling. *How could anyone hang lights that high?* My eyes caught on the sea of wings fluttering in front of me, and I had to laugh at myself. Obviously, one of the hundred *älva* in the room had flown them there.

Hold on. A hundred? And this is just part *of the settlement?*

"When you said family, I thought you meant a wife, maybe a couple of kids." Viggo's head swiveled from left to right. "But this is a small village."

"This cave houses half of the Northern Faerie Corps —a collection of *älva* who banded together in the wake of the cullings." Rafe gestured around the cavern. "We refused to subject our families to the government camps, so we came here and created our own colonies. There's another one farther north, and two in the south."

"That must mean there are hundreds of *älva* in Alfheim." I shook my head. "I thought there were only a few of us."

"Wow." Viggo's mouth hadn't fully closed since we'd arrived. "I had no idea."

"Then we've done our job." Rafe rested one hand on the hilt of his sword. "We didn't know if, or when, the government would stop abusing us for our powers. So we deemed it best to remain hidden until we could be certain our freedom was secure."

"I'm not sure if it's safe even now," I admitted. "I'm not sure what you've heard, but even with two regents, we're having a hard time effecting the changes we want to. This horrible man named Fyrs Narrik is Minister of State. And he—"

"I'm familiar with Fyrs." Rafe's knuckles whitened around his sword. "He was in my class at the academy."

"You might be thinking of someone else," I said. "This guy's *way* older than you."

"*Älva* age considerably better than light elves." Rafe shrugged.

Viggo and I exchanged looks. *Good to know.*

"Well, Narrik rose to power after the queen's

daughter—my mom—was killed. Everyone blamed the queen for all of the bad things that happened here, and she's certainly not innocent. But Narrik is the real reason things are so awful. Constance is just his puppet."

Rafe turned to me. "Now that you're also the regent, can't you have him removed from office?"

Why did everyone have to ask that?

"A change of that nature requires the support of either the senate or the cabinet," I explained. "And since all of the *sane* senators are missing, and the cabinet's under Narrik's control, I can't do anything."

"Your senators are missing?" Rafe released his sword to rub the back of his neck. "When did that happen?"

"They were abducted early last fall," Viggo answered. "There was an important vote—one that would affect the future leadership of the realm. The *Opprør* were taken the night before, and haven't returned. That's actually why we're here—we knew there were caves, and we were hoping . . ."

"You thought they might have been hidden here," Rave finished. "Let me guess—your conventional tracking methods have been ineffective?"

"Correct," Viggo confirmed.

Rafe studied me thoughtfully. "Let me ask you something. Your trackers . . . are they able to see through both kinds of blockers?"

"I'm not sure what you mean," I said. "My advisors told me both warriors and *Protektors* are out looking.

And they questioned all of Narrik's sympathizers, but so far nobody's admitted to anything."

"I see." Rafe scanned the cavern. His eyes settled on the far corner. "Have you performed energetic scans on the realm?"

"The *Empati* have run checks, but . . ." I shrugged. "Nothing's turned up."

"Mmm-hmm." Rafe's gaze hadn't shifted. "And have they run *dark* scans?"

Crazy älva said what? "I'm sorry?"

"Dark scans—searches designed to see through protections *not* native to the light realm."

"I'm sure they scanned for everything," I hedged. "My understanding is that *Empati* can spot any blocker. Those originating from a dark entity carry one signature, and those from light entities carry another. When they identify either of those, they can put a trace on the location, and work on figuring out how to disable it."

"Yes," Rafe said carefully. "But what of blockers set by *neutral* entities? Energetic warriors with fealty to neither the dark nor the light realms?"

Viggo's torso stiffened at my side. "Like a mercenary?"

"More along the lines of someone who sees the benefit in learning to utilize *both* sides of the energetic coin, and employing it for the greatest good of all. I have an idea." Rafe walked down the steps that led to the cavern. He motioned for us, and Viggo and I hurried after him.

We continued in silence, weaving through the

throng of wings and bodies and smells. A few of the adults shot us curious looks, but the kids didn't seem to notice we were there. They ran across our path, too intent on chasing balls and each other to realize there were newcomers in their top secret settlement.

My stomach rumbled as the savory tang of meat hit my nostrils. I stared longingly at the buffet just a few feet away from the path we walked. It was loaded with breads and meats and vegetables and fruits and what I could only assume was elephant-sheep cheese. We must have been honing in on dinnertime . . . and my academy-scheduled stomach hadn't been fed since breakfast.

"Viggo," I hissed. I tilted my head toward the food table. "Any chance you can snag some of that? It's on your side."

"Rafe's carrying a sword thicker than my arm," Viggo whispered back. "Do you really want me to mess with him?"

"Kind of," I admitted. "I'm hungry. And he said he'd feed us, right?"

Rafe hung a right at the end of the aisle. With one last longing glance at my would-be meal, I followed him to the far side of the room. Viggo slipped his hand around mine as Rafe stopped in front of a large drafting table. A winged girl hunched over the desk, sketching intently. Long, dark hair with indigo high-lights hung over one side of her face, obscuring it from view. The side I could see was scrunched in concentration. Her emerald eyes narrowed as she moved her pencil across the paper.

"Maja," Rafe said softly.

The girl didn't look up.

"Maja," Rafe said, this time placing his hand atop her arm.

She jumped, her pencil leaving a trail of grey across the drawing. "Dad! What?"

"Maja," Raja's voice carried a slight edge. "I want to introduce you to someone."

His daughter tilted her head. She glanced quickly at Viggo, but as she tucked her hair behind her shoulder, her eyes settled on me. I'd been off about their color. Instead of being pure emerald like Rafe's and Viggo's, Maja's pupils were surrounded by a rim of a different hue, one that was almost purple. Her ivory skin covered her angular cheekbones, and each of her ears were decorated with silver cuffs and rings. They matched the silver ribbons she'd braided into her hair. Her wings, the same silver shade as Viggo's, glittered like her father's. And though her frame was slight, her arms carried the telltale muscles of someone whose life depended on being able to take care of themselves.

Maja was one badass *älva*.

"Viggo, Aura. This is my daughter. Maja, this is your cousin, Viggo. And Aura, Alfheim's new ruler."

"Co-ruler," I corrected. "And it's nice to meet you."

"New ruler." Maja's eyes narrowed. "And will you carry on the practice of forcing *älva* to serve *the greater good*?"

Viggo's hand tightened around mine.

"I was unaware of that practice until today," I said calmly. "But it's certainly not one I endorse. Nor do I intend to allow it to continue."

"Is that so?" Maja challenged.

"Absolutely."

Maja stared at me for what felt like forever. I held my ground, unwilling to show how unnerved I was by her indigo-emerald glare. Maybe walking into a cavern filled with refugees who had a justifiable bone to pick with my grandmother hadn't been my brightest idea.

I shifted the hand not holding Viggo's to the hilt of my dagger. Maja watched the movement, then shrugged. She picked up her pencil, and resumed drawing.

My eyes sought out Viggo's. *Is that it?*

"Maja." Rafe plucked the pencil from her hand. She pinned him with an irritated glare that would have intimidated the Helheim out of me, but seemed to be a non-issue to her father. "You need to welcome your cousin and your queen."

"Co-ruler," I corrected again. "Just call me Aura. Really."

Maja leaned back in her chair. "And why would I do that?"

"Because we need them to help us free those we've lost," Rafe said. "And they need you to help them free their politicians."

Her? Don't they have somebody else who could help us? Maybe someone just a little less hostile?

Maja snorted. "If politicians are trapped some-where, how is that a bad thing?"

"Because these politicians will vote in alignment with our beliefs," Rafe explained. "They can return Alfheim to the realm it once was."

Maja's snark slipped slightly. "A realm where we could go anywhere?"

"Yes," Rafe said quietly.

"All of us. Including Emilie? Would she be free again?"

My throat tightened. "Who's Emilie?"

"My sister." Maja's eyes blazed. "She was taken to the camps over a year ago. She was patrolling our southern border, and she crossed the barrier to deter a trespasser. It turned out to be a soldier—one who, apparently, would earn a big reward for capturing another *älva*. My sister's patrol partner heard the exchange over her communicator, but she wasn't able to reach her in time. Emilie was bound and the trans-port had gone before Fila got halfway to her station."

Icicles traipsed my spine. "That's terrible."

"It is," Maja said coldly. "So, forgive me if I'm not overly excited to meet you, Your Majesty."

"Hey. That's not fair," I said. "I had nothing to do with any of that."

"But you haven't done anything to fix it, have you?"

"She didn't know." Viggo's voice was a low rumble. "Neither of us did. Listen, we're sorry for your loss. Truly, we are. But you need to get that Aura's trying to create a different Alfheim—one where *everyone* is free to be who they are, without fear and without judgment. It's horrible that your sister was taken, but if you want her back, you'll get off Aura's case and get on our side."

Maja's eyes narrowed before she shifted her gaze to me. It took everything I had to not blink.

"Fine," Maja finally said. "I'm in."

I glanced at Viggo. "In?"

"I'll help you," Maja said slowly. "But it doesn't mean I want anything else to do with you."

"I . . . uh . . ." I closed my mouth. I had no idea what to think about this girl.

Viggo crossed his arms. "You don't like us."

"No," Maja said. "I don't."

"You don't know us," I pointed out.

Maja flipped one of her silver-ribboned braids over her shoulder. "Viggo. My cousin. You're an *älva* with an unnatural blend of light and dark energy. You're a full-blood, so the darkness isn't genetic; it must come from time spent off-realm. You're fiercely protective, possess a sizeable ego, and have an inexplicable link to *her.*" Maja jutted her chin at me, before closing her eyes. "You're either her defender, or her . . . *ew.* You're mates?"

My eyes widened. How did she get all of that?

"Were you briefed before we arrived?" I glanced around. Was there some Eunice equivalent in *älva* country?

"I didn't have to be." Maja rolled her eyes. "And you. Aura the ruler. You have an unusual blend of light and dark as well. You're *not* full-blooded, so that darkness may actually be genetic." She closed her eyes. "Oh, that's rich. Our new ruler is part dark elf? And she claims to be here to help us?"

"I am here to help you." I spoke through gritted teeth.

"If you say so." Maja opened her eyes. "You're insecure, unsure how to handle your darkness, and you're absolutely terrified of failing as miserably as the ruler before you. There. Now I know you."

"Maja," Rafe hissed.

I raised my hand. "No. She's right." *Freakishly right.* "How did you figure all of that out?"

Maja shrugged. "I read you."

I narrowed my eyes. "Are you an *Empati?*"

"We don't get fancy titles here," Maja said.

"Can you control energy?" I rephrased.

"Yes." Maja snatched her pencil from Rafe. "Now can I get back to work?"

Rafe let out an exasperated sigh. "Maja does control energy. But not in the way an *Empati*, or a dark elf might. She is a genetic contradiction—half *älva*, half Svartish. Her mother is from the dark realm."

My breath caught in my throat. "She's like me."

Maja's nostrils flared. "I'm nothing like you. I'm well aware of who I am, and what I'm here to do."

"And who are you?" Viggo asked.

"I'm Maja Sorenssön." She raised her chin proudly. "I protect our homeland with blockers that have never been broken, and curses that are impenetrable . . . though clearly, I'll need to rework the formulation on whichever one you managed to glitch through. I am the protector of the Northern Faerie Corps, and the liaison between all of our branches."

"And *what* are you?" Viggo pressed.

"In that, I *am* just like Aura." My heart stilled as Maja looked me dead in the eye. "I'm a dark faerie."

CHAPTER 12

"I'M SORRY. I'M NOT a dark anything." I shook my head.

"You're a halfling. Half *älva*, half dark elf. Same as me." Maja stared me down.

"Aura's the crown princess of a light realm," Viggo said calmly. "No matter what her genetics, she's light. Period."

"Tell yourself whatever you want." Maja shrugged. "It's just a label, anyway."

"Labels can get you killed around here." My voice wavered, and I bit on the inside of my cheek.

"You think I don't know that?" Maja leaned forward, her eyes blazing. "I've spent my entire life mapping out every conceivable way to keep *your* government away from *my* family. My parents built the colony itself, but I'm the one who's protected it with curses, blockers, and energetic weapons your warriors have never even heard of. While you've been running around your precious palace, enjoying your freedom, I've been developing acid clouds and crystal barriers so my people can have a semblance of a normal life. So, don't talk to me about the dangers of labels. *Princess.*"

Viggo shifted so he stood slightly in front of me. His hand once again gripped his dagger. "I think we should leave."

"Maybe we should," I gritted.

"Go ahead." Maja turned her attention back to her drawing. "It's not like you were actually going to help us, anyway."

"Maja," Rafe admonished. "That's quite enough."

I winced as my molars pierced my cheek. Releasing my bite, I moved beside Viggo. "What is your problem with me?"

"You're weak." Maja resumed her sketching. "You're actually in a position to make a difference, but you're too scared to do anything about it."

"Watch it." Viggo's tone carried a hint of a threat. "Aura's traveled hundreds of miles to track *literally anything* that will help us find our missing senators—the ones who can kick Narrik out of office, and restore our realm before it destroys itself. She fought off a dark elf and a Huldra and forced the queen to accept her as an equal. She is the farthest thing from weak, and if you know what's good for you, you'll apologize to her *right now.*"

Maja's eyes flickered. "Are you done?"

A low growl erupted from Viggo's throat, but I placed my hand on his arm. "This is a dead end. She doesn't have any idea where our senators are, and we're losing time. Rafe, I'm sorry to have bothered you. If you hear anything about where the missing might be, send word to the academy."

I turned on one heel and walked away.

"I never said I don't know where your senators are." Maja's words brought me to a stop.

"Excuse me?"

"You heard me."

My wings stilled and I rotated slowly. "If you have information about our senators, you have to tell us."

"They're in the south—in a cave not far from our sister colony. But you'll never be able to get to them. You aren't strong enough."

"Watch me," I ground out.

"Please." Maja pointed one black-polished fingernail. "You can barely use your light powers. How are you going to get past the dark blockers?"

Crêpes. The senators were behind dark blockers?

"How do you know what Aura can do?" Viggo challenged.

"Because she's an open freaking book." Maja rolled her eyes. "I've been reading energy signatures since I was a baby. And hers is practically screaming with desperation. The potential is there—in fact, it's greater than any I've seen before, besides mine of course. But it's untapped and underdeveloped. Whatever they're teaching you in that palace isn't going to do a thing against the entities that are moving on Alfheim."

"If you're aware of a threat to the realm, disclosing it would benefit us *both*," I said.

"It would," Maja agreed. "But I've seen what your government does when faced with a perceived threat. You'll forgive me if I don't subject my family to servitude."

Rafe stepped forward to tap the desk. "This schematic Maja is working on . . . it's intended to be an extractor. One we've planned to use on our members being held within the camps. It requires significant power—more than Maja, or any of our residents possess on their own. If you are as strong as Maja believes you can be, perhaps combining your powers might be enough to break the hold and free our brothers and sisters."

"It would take years to get her to the level she'd need to be." Maja rolled her eyes. "And like she said, she's just wasting her time here."

"I'll do it," I said. "I'll study, or train, or do whatever it takes to help you free the *älva*. But in exchange, you have to help us extract our senators, too."

Viggo stood steady at my side.

Maja's eyes narrowed. "You'd be willing to tap into your Svartish side? Develop your dark gifts, as well as your light ones?"

"As I said." I crossed my arms. "I'll do whatever it takes to help my people."

Maja's eyes flashed, and for a second I glimpsed a

flicker of something that looked suspiciously like hope. But in a blink it was gone, replaced with Maja's signature scowl.

"Whatever." She resumed her drawing. "Let me know when you're ready."

"I'm ready," I declared.

My stomach rumbled in dissent.

"You're hungry," Rafe deduced. "You both must be. Come. We'll get you fed and settled into one of our vacant residential quarters. Your work with my daughter may take some time."

"We don't have much," I said. "The longer our senators are missing, the sicker our realm gets."

"Then Maja will work quickly to teach you," Rafe said. "Won't she?"

"Yes," Maja muttered without glancing up.

"Good. Now, come with me. I'll show you where we eat, and introduce you to the rest of my family. The *more polite* members." Rafe patted Maja's back, and walked toward the banquet. With one more glance at the girl who seemed to hate me, I laced my fingers through Viggo's and followed Rafe through the cavern.

Something told me I'd taken on more than I'd bargained for.

Later that night, Viggo and I were sprawled across the two couches in our temporary living quarters. Rafe had put us in a two-bedroom suite adjacent to Maja's, and even my proximity to the broody girl couldn't dampen my awe at the level of luxury these *älva* had managed to bring to a cave. I'd expected the quarters to be sparse—rough walls, plenty of darkness, maybe a mat for a bed. Instead, Viggo and I now lounged in the equivalent of a Midgardian five-star hotel. Thick, downy comforters sat atop the four-poster beds that took the place of honor in each bedroom. The living area had two full-length couches that framed a dark-wood coffee table, and a small dining table that was nestled against an actual living wall—one lined from floor to ceiling with ivy, moss, and flowering green plants, the likes of which I'd never seen back home. And while the rest of the walls were indeed carved out of stone, they were illuminated with sconces bearing flameless candles. A chandelier hung from the center of the living area, its own lights adjusting their intensity whenever Viggo or I said the words *brighten* or *dim.* I doubted there was any kind of electricity running through the rocks, which meant the lights were powered by whatever kind of magic ran inside the faeries' wings. *Are Viggo and I going to get that power? Better talk to Rafe about it.*

Later.

The day had fully exhausted me. After we'd eaten, Rafe had introduced us to his wife, Syrra, and the rest of the warriors that made up his council. The Northern Faerie Corps was governed by a group of elected advisors. Unlike Alfheim's government, there was no singular leader, nor was there a senate to overrule major decisions. Instead, the council reached accords through a vote, effecting policies beneficial to the entirety of the colony with minimal drama. It was a streamlined process—one that had worked for the faeries so far.

Could we implement something equally simple at the capital?

Dare to dream, Aura.

"Hey." Viggo spoke from the other couch. I glanced over to find him flat on his back, one arm draped over the cushions. "We should probably check in with Elin and Finna. I'm about to pass out."

I rolled my head to the side. "You call them. Eight hours of flying made me too beat to move."

I closed my eyes, the familiar tapping sound confirming that Viggo was doing the connecting for us. A half-minute later, the room was filled with a light buzz. I opened my eyes to find the holographic image of Elin and Finna huddled close together.

"There you are. We were worried—you said you'd check in after dinner!" Elin chastised.

"It is after dinner," I called.

"Aura? I can't see you." Finna craned her neck.

"That's because the princess is too tired to rise from her couch," Viggo retorted.

"I told you not to call me that," I grumbled. But his words had their desired effect. I pushed myself up and shuffled the short distance to sit beside him. "Hey."

"Yikes." Elin leaned closer. "What happened to you?"

"Flew eight hours, met Viggo's uncle, discovered

there's another dark faerie, checked into a fancy cave hotel." I shrugged. "The usual."

"Hold on." Elin raised one hand. "What do you mean *another* dark fae—?"

"Viggo has an uncle?" Finna interrupted. "Oh, gods. Is he anything like your uncle?"

"Forget all of that." Jande elbowed his way into the frame. "Tell me about the upscale cave hotel!"

"Hey, Jande." Viggo nodded. "Any word from Ondyr?"

"He and Zara got to their destination at midday," Jande said. "They've been running recon, but nothing's turned up so far."

"What's their strategy?" I asked.

"They've made camp for the night, and they'll search more in the morning—which we know because *they* checked in after dinner, as discussed." Elin arched one brow.

"Sorry," I muttered.

"So, they haven't found anything?" Viggo pressed his back against the couch. "No leads?"

"No leads," Finna confirmed. "They haven't even made contact with anyone. Apparently, where they are, it's completely barren."

Viggo glanced at me. "If they don't have anything by morning, call them home. Our sources here say what we're looking for is in the south—near this camp's sister colony."

Elin's spine straightened. "Are the senators being held by *älva*?"

"I don't think so." I leaned into Viggo.

"Then how do your sources know where they are?" Finna asked. "Wait, is Viggo's uncle your source? Is he trustworthy? No offense, Viggo."

"None taken." Viggo shrugged. "And I think so. Though since I hadn't met him before today . . . that I remember anyway . . . who knows?"

"He's a good guy," I said quickly. "I don't get any bad vibes from him. His daughter, however . . ."

"Is she the dark faerie?" Elin asked. "Is *she* like your uncle, Aura?"

"No," I said firmly. "She's got issues, for sure. But she's no Dragen."

"What exactly is a dark faerie?" Jande piped up.

"She's half *älva*, half dark elf. Like me," I said quietly.

"Not quite." Viggo slung his arm around my shoulders. "She's lacking your signature pluck."

I shot him the side-eye. "Pluck?"

"Your undeterred optimism," Viggo explained. "Even in the face of near-certain failure."

"Rude."

Viggo shrugged. "Not many girls would have agreed to break through a dark blocker, without any training."

"Hold on." Elin raised both palms. "Aura, what is he talking about? What did you agree to do?"

"Let's rewind. It's kind of a lot." I quickly caught our academy friends up on what Viggo and I had learned that day—about the *älva* being held in camps, their tie to Viggo's family, and the existence of a secondary faerie colony to the south . . . not too far from the alleged location of our missing officials.

"So, you have to help this chick free her sister, and then she'll help us save our senators?" Elin crossed her arms.

"Pretty much."

Finna pursed her lips. "I don't like it, Aura. It sounds dangerous."

"What about our lives *isn't* dangerous?" I sighed. "If there's a chance she's right about where and how our senators are being concealed, we have to at least try. I can't break through that kind of blocker on my own, and our full-blown *Empati* haven't even been able to *spot* it. How are they supposed to locate the *Opprør* behind a barricade they can't even see?"

"Maja seems to be offering the only tangible solution," Viggo confirmed. "But I'm with you, Finna. I don't like Aura being on the line either. I'll be with her the entire time, and if I think things are going too far I'll extract her. You have my word."

"You're sure you can do that alone?" Finna asked Viggo. "Do you want us to have Signy send in our warriors?"

"I don't think our hosts would approve of that," I said. "They're super private. They have all these protections set around their colony. An acid cloud almost ate us on the way in."

"Seriously?" Jande balked.

"Yup," I confirmed. "We'll let you know if we need support. I honestly think the best thing we can do is prove to the *älva* that we're on their side. There are a lot of them, and they're pretty intense warriors from what I can see."

"And the dark faerie?" Elin's eyes narrowed. "Viggo, you'll make sure she doesn't pull any fast ones?"

"I've got Aura's back," Viggo confirmed. "Always."

"Okay," Elin said grudgingly. "What's your plan?"

"I'm going to train with Maja—figure out how to break though the different kinds of dark blockers that might be in place." I looked over at Viggo. "It's probably going to take a few days, so we'll check in morning and night with updates."

"I'll run communications for us. And yes," he said as Elin opened her mouth, "I promise I'll follow your schedule."

"After breakfast and dinner," Elin reminded him. "If you're late, I'm sending an alarm to your comm."

"I'd expect nothing less." Viggo didn't crack a smile.

"We'll recall Ondyr and Zara in the morning," Elin said. "Hopefully they learn something while they're there. It'd be good to have a full picture of what we're going against. Or who. Jeez. We still have no idea who's behind this."

"Do the *älva* have any insights?" Finna asked.

"Not that I'm aware of, but we'll definitely ask," I said. "I get the impression Maja sees more than she lets on."

"Stay on her good side," Finna warned.

I rested my head against Viggo's shoulder and stifled a yawn. "I plan to."

Viggo gave my leg a light squeeze. "We'd better go. It's been a long day."

"Check in after breakfast," Elin ordered.

Viggo brought two fingers to his forehead in a salute. "Tell Ondyr and Zara to get some rest. Sounds like our next move is going to be intense."

"Be safe," Finna said. "Both of you."

"We will." This time I couldn't stop the yawn that overtook me. I covered my mouth as I said, "You too."

We signed off, Viggo pressing the button on his comm before turning his attention to me. "You about ready to turn in?"

"I am," I said. "But there was a lot to unpack today. Are you okay with all of this? Finding out you have a family, and they have an entire colony . . . plus your cousin's half dark like me? That's got to be weird."

"For the hundredth time, there is no weirdness in you being who you are." Viggo shook his head. "Your Svartalfheim side isn't bad. It's just a place, Aura. Who you are is up to you."

"I get that," I said. And I did. "But all of this would be a lot to take in for anyone. How are you?"

"Happy to find out I'm not the only Sorenssön," Viggo said honestly. "Meeting my dad's brother is like having a piece of him back again. Or, it could be. I don't know much about Rafe, except that he runs this place and he's kept everyone hidden all this time. Seems to be a decent guy so far."

"He does." I nestled my head against Viggo's chest. "And having access to an entire group of *älva* is a huge asset. If they can keep their colony off Narrik's radar for this long, they must be really fierce."

Viggo and I sat in silence. My thoughts drifted from the acid cloud to the dead forest to the dust I suspected powered Rafe's subterfuge.

"Do you think we're going to get that magic faerie powder stuff?" I asked. "Will we be able to illuminate rooms and do . . . whatever it does?"

"*Älva* dust? I hope so." Viggo tucked an errant strand behind my ear. "Think of everything we could get done with that. Forget resolutions—we could magic everything the way it's supposed to be."

My spine stiffened. "Do you think that's possible?"

"No idea. But if Narrik had camps, you can bet the dust—and *älva* in general—are more powerful than we were led to believe."

I bit on my bottom lip. "Why do I get the feeling there's a *lot* about us that we never knew?"

"Good thing we're in a place to get some answers." Viggo pushed himself to his feet and held out his palm. "Come on. I'm exhausted."

I placed my hand in his, and followed him across the living room. When we reached my door, he bent to plant a chaste kiss on my cheek.

"That's it?" I set my hand on my hip.

"Goodnight, *Glitre*." Viggo chuckled. "We've got another big day ahead of us."

I reluctantly closed my door, and changed into the silky pajama set our hosts had left on my bed. This place really was the height of luxury.

But as I lay in my king-sized four-poster, I couldn't block the worry from crowding my mind. In the morning I'd be training with a dark faerie, opening myself to powers I'd never even known I had. As much as this would help Maja's cause, and if I was lucky, the rest of Alfheim, I couldn't help but wonder . . .

What exactly had I signed on to do?

CHAPTER 13

THE NEXT FORTY-EIGHT hours were a crash course in energy. By the end of my second full day with Maja, I could have written a textbook: *Everything I Never Knew I Never Knew.* Professor Asling's auras and chakras class, once the bane of my academic existence, had been a walk in the park compared to Maja's trial by dark-magic fire. I'd quickly learned that drawing on the *other* side of my abilities required an entirely different access point. While Signy and Professor Asling had trained me to draw light energy from the center of the realm and channel it through the seven centers along my spine, Maja taught me to pull dark energy from an external source. I wasn't clear whether it originated from Svartalfheim, where my dad had been born, or from Helheim itself. But when I'd opened myself up, it came at me like a horde of angry bees, jabbing intently at the edge of my aura until I parted my blocker and let it in.

Before doing so, I'd taken extra care to fortify my protections—anchor myself to the realm, fill my centers with light, and mentally gird my bubble in case immediate, forcible bee ejection was necessary. It hadn't taken me long to figure out that dark energy was no joke. The first time I'd let it in, I'd been filled with such desolate despair, it took an hour for Viggo to talk me off the ground. The second time, I'd been so overcome with rage that I very nearly ripped Maja's arm off. And the third, I'd encountered a trio of terrifying entities within the confines of my mind—a dark elf, a demon, and a bizarro version of my grandmother, each goading me to use my newly accessed power to destroy the colony, and everyone within it.

After that, I learned to limit the amount of darkness I let in. No way was I going to be responsible for the fall of a quarter of Alfheim's *älva* population . . . no matter how much Maja made me want to punch her.

As promised, my surly counterpart was doing her best to teach me. She'd shown me how to access the bees, which centers to run them through for maximum effect, and had created some simple blockers for me to dismantle. I'd broken through both the dark crystal and the acid fog blockers, but the clearing columns left me baffled. Maja had designed her extraction schematic to overpower them—apparently under the guidance of more than one able-bodied dual energy worker. But while Maja demonstrated an admirable level of competence, the columns remained well above my pay grade.

"I can't do it," I panted as I shot my hundredth hand

beam into a seeming abyss. Viggo was somewhere in the meadow, concealed by four columns that simultaneously held him captive and cloaked his location. "Viggo, just come out already. I'm never going to release you."

"Blocker down," Maja called.

My boyfriend emerged from thin air. He climbed two unseen stairs to step into the grassy meadow. "You were close," he offered. "The columns were starting to crack at the edges."

"Yeah, but they didn't." I dropped onto the grass and lowered my head to me knees. "We should just call it a day, Maja. This one's too hard for me."

"Only because you think it is. Get up," Maja ordered. Her black cloak fluttered around her legs as she held out a hand. "Try again."

"I've tried fifteen times," I groaned. "I can feel it's there, but I can't break through the shield hiding Viggo."

"You need to shift your mindset." Maja wrapped her hand around mine and pulled me to my feet. "You're trying so hard to keep the darkness from overtaking you that you're not letting enough of it in."

"Yeah, well, you didn't see Bizarro Constance," I muttered. "She's even scarier than the real one."

"Then use her." Maja released me, and flexed her hands, waving them through the air in front of my body. "Use *all* of the things that frighten you. Intolerance, destruction, Narrik, spiders . . . huh. What are clowns?"

"Ugh. These creepy things Midgardians bring out for birthday parties. Hey." I placed my hands on my hips. "How'd you know I was scared of clowns? Did you scan me?"

"Somebody has to do something, or we're never getting any sleep." Maja tilted her head at the indigo sky. We'd been working for so long that dusk now blanketed the meadow.

"Fine. What do you suggest?" I brushed the grass from my palms and squared off against the invisible columns. They were out there somewhere, nestled among the sleeping sheep.

Lucky sheep.

"You can feel the blocker, right?" Maja asked.

I raised my hands and waited until tiny needles pinged against my palms. "Yup. But I can't break through it."

"Enough with the can'ts. Thoughts hold power, and you're ceding yours to incompetence."

"Hey." I crossed my arms.

"Am I wrong?" Maja challenged.

I bit back my retort. "Once I feel the blocker, what do I do?"

"Call in *both* of your energies—the light and the dark. Draw the light in through your feet, and the dark through your palms."

"I've been doing that. It doesn't do what you—"

"I wasn't done," Maja interrupted. "Once you've let in equal parts of both, allow them to mix. If you've blended correctly they'll form a double helix, the light and the dark intermingling until they bond together to form a third energy—a neutral energy."

I closed my eyes and did as Maja instructed. The angry bees jabbed at my space, rushing in and smothering the light until it was barely discernable. Bizarro Constance appeared in front of me, her bony fingers reaching out as if she intended to choke me.

"It's too much dark," I gritted. "Let me just—"

"It's not enough dark." Maja countered. "Let in more."

"No! She'll kill me!"

"Let. In. More." Maja placed her hands on my shoulders. "I'll guide it into place."

"Aura?" Viggo's voice carried an edge. "You okay?"

"I won't let it hurt her," Maja promised. "But she has to get over this edge. Let it in."

With a deep breath, I did as Maja instructed. A second surge of black bees flew at the light, entwining it in a cloud of darkness. My throat clenched, and nausea roiled in my gut. But Maja's hands pressed against my shoulders, and a calming stream filled my body. I breathed through my discomfort, and the black swarm morphed into a dizzying, grey spiral. The light expanded, gradually overtaking the dark until a shimmering, silvery helix spun inside of me.

What the actual Helheim?

"That's the balance you need to draw," Maja said. "Now, Viggo, step inside the columns. Once you're in place, Aura will break them down."

With my eyes closed, I couldn't see what was

happening in the meadow. But soft footsteps let me know that Viggo was on the move. And when I raised my palms to the place Maja had set the columns, I sensed his comforting presence somewhere on the other side. "Now?" I asked.

"Now," Maja confirmed. She released her hold on me, and I drew a slow breath.

Here goes nothing.

I focused on the double helix in my chest, pulling lightly on its strands and channeling it through my arms. Sparks burst from my hands like a garden hose on full blast. My mind saw the energy split into four streams, attacking each of the columns and hammering at them until cracks began to form. My arms trembled as the columns split apart and tumbled to the earth. When I opened my eyes, Viggo stood slack jawed atop a shimmering platform on the grass. The remains of the columns glittered in dust-like particles all around him.

"Whoa," Viggo whispered.

"Seriously," I whispered back.

"And *that* is how you dismantle a clearing column." Maja patted my shoulder. "About time. Think you can do that again tomorrow? For real, this time?"

My heart hammered. "You want to try the rescue tomorrow?"

"I've wanted to do it for months, but I haven't been able to do it on my own. Apparently, it takes two dark faeries to create enough power to pull this off." Maja shrugged. "We'll make a remote attempt in the morning. If it's unsuccessful, we'll reevaluate our strategy."

"What happens if we're successful?" I asked cautiously. "Won't there be physical restraints holding everyone in the camp, too?"

"Of course there will be." Maja rolled her eyes. "But *älva* are fighters. They'll be able to overpower any guards. It's the columns we haven't been able to break through. My mom and I weren't strong enough—not even when we tried together. But you're next level fierce with this energy, Aura—maybe because you're a dark faerie with noble blood?"

"And a Key," Viggo said.

Maja shrugged. "Either way, the two of us we should be able to manage it."

Viggo moved closer. "It's probably more than just guards holding them. You've scanned the area—what exactly do you know about their environment?"

Maja crossed her arms. "During the day they're held in an open-aired unit—a vast space enclosed by containment columns. The columns arch into a dome, forming a complete casing so they can't escape. Guards circle the perimeter, armed with weapons ranging from swords—which, obviously, could be overtaken— to stunners, which pose more of a problem. And of course, there are longer-range weapons stationed at each corner of the compound."

"Compound?" I asked.

"The whole camp is surrounded by an enormous stone wall," Maja said. "It may be a castle."

"Jeez." How had something this big been operating without my being aware of it?

"The easiest time to make our move will be during the morning transfer—when the *älva* are being moved from their bunks to the work unit. If we're fast, we'll only need to break the columns encasing the castle itself. If not, we'll have the second set to deal with."

"What happens after you and Aura break the columns?" Viggo asked. "Do you have any way to fill your sister in on what's happening?"

"No," Maja said. "But unlike light elves, who remain abysmally thick-headed, *älva* evolved to be highly intuitive. Emilie will sense the shift in energy. Once it's reached a certain level, she'll know to take off."

"I hope so," I said cautiously. "But why count on that when you have additional resources that could *ensure* this mission's success?"

Maja frowned. "What are you talking about?"

"I'm talking about getting help." I pointed to the communicator on my wrist. "It's time to bring in the troops."

CHAPTER 14

"THE TROOPS?" MAJA'S BROW rose.

"Let me bring my aunt in on this," I said. "She's my *Protektor*, so she's got access to some of our realm's best warriors."

"They're on our side," Viggo interjected as Maja opened her mouth. "Signy wouldn't call on anyone who wasn't."

Maja stared at me, as if sizing up my own trustworthiness. "Okay," she finally said. "Call her."

I tapped Signy's sequence into my comm. We'd spoken briefly the day before, so she knew where I was and what I was doing. But I doubted she'd be thrilled that we'd spontaneously decided to orchestrate a jailbreak . . . or that I'd need her to work through the night to organize the extraction team we required to make it happen.

Though she'd do anything to get our senators back.

"Aura?" Signy's hologram appeared above my

communicator. Her forehead was etched with frown lines, and she wore the gaunt face of someone who'd been awake for days. "Did something happen?"

"No. I'm still fine," I reassured her. "I'm here with Viggo and Maja, and we've got a big ask for you."

"Anything. How can I help?" Signy's fingers worried the handle of a mug in front of her.

"Remember how I told you about Maja's sister, and the rest of the *älva* being held near the capital?"

"Yes." Signy's brows formed a *V.* "Constance's failure to disclose that to us is something we'll be dealing with at our next session."

"I'm counting on it," I said. "But hopefully we'll be doing it from a better place. We're going to try to free them soon."

"How soon? Are you on your way home?" Signy asked.

"No. Maja figured out a way to lift the blockers holding the *älva* prisoners. It's something we can do remotely, but . . ."

"But we're going to need a team on the ground to make sure there aren't any additional barriers in our way," Viggo jumped in. "Maja thinks the prisoners can overpower guards, but we aren't sure if there are any weapons in place."

"And you need to knock out anything an *älva* can't disable," Signy deduced. "I can make that happen. How soon do you need us in place?"

I glanced at Viggo. "Can you secure the site by dawn?"

"As in, tomorrow at dawn?" Signy's brows shot to her forehead. "Do you even know where they're being held?"

"Not exactly," I hemmed. "Maja says they're in a structure that looks like a castle, about a hundred miles south of the palace."

"Constance has a summer residence near that location," Signy said. "It backs up to a mountain range. Could that be it?"

"Maja?" I turned to Viggo's cousin. She'd closed her eyes, and was either meditating or sleeping. "Um, Maja?"

"Is there a lake on the western edge of that castle?" Maja didn't open her eyes.

"Yes." Surprise colored Signy's voice. "How did you—"

"I'm looking at it. That's the one." Maja's eyes flew open. "The mountains hide a series of tunnels that lead to a cavern big enough to hold them all. They can evacuate to there—I'll cloak the entrance so the guards can't find them. Once it's safe to relocate, we can bring them home."

Viggo leaned in to study the hologram. "What do you think, Professor Bergen? Can you get a team in place by morning?"

"It'll be tight," Signy said. "But it's not impossible. Larkin's unit just returned from an off-realm mission. They should be able to assist."

Viggo nodded. "That'd be great."

"Why now?" Signy asked. "Wouldn't it be more

prudent to wait a few days? Make sure everything's airtight?"

"Um . . ." I glanced at the raven-haired girl by my side. Maja played with her cuticles, her lips turned down in a frown.

"Because my sister is being held there." Maja's voice wavered. It was the first time I'd heard so much as a hint of vulnerability from the steel-willed faerie.

"Oh, sweet girl." Signy's warmth emanated through the comm. "I'm so sorry to hear it."

"Thank you," Maja said quietly.

"Maja's been working on a way to free her sister—and the others—for months. Our teaming up is a huge breakthrough, and she wants to move before the opportunity disappears." In other words, before someone caught on to what we were doing . . . or I came to my senses about the risks of dabbling with dark energy and reneged on our arrangement.

Shudder.

Viggo squeezed my hand.

"Besides," he added, "we believe the senators may be being held in a similar setup. If we can break though this one, we'll be better equipped to handle our next extraction."

"Say no more." Signy raised her hand. "Viggo, send me any additional mission details as soon as you can. I'll go speak to Larkin now, and secure her unit's availability."

"Thanks, Signy." I smiled at the hologram. "I can always count on you."

"Forever," she said. "But stay safe, all right? Viggo, if anything happens to Aura—"

"I've got her back," he assured her. "And Maja's, too."

The faerie looked over with a start.

"We're cousins." Viggo shrugged. "I may not be able to do the whole dark energy thing, but I'm not too bad with a sword."

"Dark energy thing?" Signy's voice cracked. "What aren't you telling me?"

"Uh, I'll fill you in at home," I said hastily. "Gotta go prep. Bye!"

"Aura," Signy warned.

"I'll be safe, I promise."

"You'd better be. All three of you." Signy shook her head as she logged off.

When her hologram disappeared, I turned to Maja. "We're all set. Though I will need as much information as you can get me. Signy's good, but she's not a mind reader. Well, not a full one at any rate."

"Here." Maja tapped something into her communicator. "That extractor drawing I was working on? It's part of a larger schematic of the location my sister's being held. I've just sent it to you, along with a second image that outlines the optimal removal strategy. You can share them with your aunt."

I glanced at my wrist. Sure enough, my comm lit with the incoming message. Viggo's did the same.

"I'll send it to Professor Bergen," he offered. "And I'll update Elin and Finna so they know what's going on."

He set to work typing, while I addressed Maja. "We'll do everything we can to help your sister," I promised. "And the rest of your people, too."

"Thanks," Maja said quietly. She looked over at me, and it was there again—that flicker of vulnerability. She opened her mouth as though she were going to say something more, but quickly snapped it shut. The next moment, she'd pushed herself to her feet, and crossed her arms. "Your satchel. What's in it?"

I fingered the small bag I'd hung from my belt loop. "They're crystals," I muttered.

"You're carrying Jande's crystals?" Viggo's lips quirked.

"I had no idea what we were walking into, and he said they'd protect me." I raised my chin defiantly. "Don't judge me."

"I'm not judging anyone." Viggo raised his palms.

"You have aventurine in there." Maja stared at the satchel. "And amethyst. And . . . is that labradorite?"

"I have no idea." I untied the satchel and held it out. "You can look."

"I am looking." Maja's eyes met mine, her expression reflecting her low opinion of my intellect.

"Right. You can read the stones' signatures through the bag. Well, take it anyway." I thrust it at her. "I don't know what half of these are."

Maya palmed the satchel. Her thin fingers parsed through its contents until she withdrew a translucent, purple stone. "Why aren't you using this?"

"I had it on my belt loop," I said defensively.

"This." She raised the stone. "*This* is what you need to help channel your energy."

"The purple one is . . . uh . . ."

"This purple one is labradorite. It comes in several colors, but this particular stone is extremely pure. And extremely powerful. Whoever gave it to you clearly knows their stuff."

"Yeah, Jande's top of his class." I squinted at the crystal. "So, what does it do? And more importantly, how does it keep me from losing it with all of that . . . stuff going on inside of me?"

"Labradorite is a protection stone. Not only does it deflect unwanted energies, but it helps you manage the energy you *are* working with. It heightens intuition, calms your mind, and most importantly, it helps transform you into the being you're meant to become."

"That little rock does all that?" Viggo blinked.

"It's a crystal," Maja said dully. "And yes. It does."

Oh.

"You need to be wearing this. *Not* on your belt loop," Maja added when I opened my mouth to object. "I'm not always going to be here to guide you, and you need an external device to help until you've mastered your abilities. I assume neither of you are skilled metalworkers?"

I glanced at Viggo. "Uh, no. Definitely not. Wait. Why? Are you?"

Maja didn't answer. "I'm taking this, and turning it into a necklace. It should be touching your skin at all times when we work. Got it?"

"Sure. Yeah. Uh, thanks?"

Maja shoved the satchel back at me. I took it, and tied it around my belt loop again.

"So, now I guess we should, um . . ."

"I'm going to bed," Maja said abruptly. "I'll come to your quarters at six a.m."

"Okay." What else could I say?

Maja turned on one heel and stalked toward the caves. "Be ready!" she called over her shoulder.

"We will," I promised.

"Goodnight," Viggo yelled after her. He shook his head as he walked to my side. "Who knew about the crystals?"

"Certainly not me. Don't tell Jande—if his head gets any bigger, it might explode."

Viggo chuckled. "Maja's something else, huh?

"Yeah." I reached to retie my ponytail. "But I would be too, if Elin was taken away. That's terrible about her sister."

"It is," Viggo agreed. "And tomorrow we'll do something about it. But you could drive yourself crazy worrying about all of these things that are beyond your control."

"I know. But it's hard." I shook my head. "And it's scary, letting that dark stuff inside. I'm afraid it'll take over and just . . ."

A shudder wracked my spine, and Viggo slipped his arms around me.

"Hey," he whispered. "You're the strongest *Verge* I know. Nothing's going to happen to you."

"You can't say that for sure." I laid my cheek against his chest, drinking in his familiar blend of cedar and calm. "What if I'm not strong enough to keep it from overpowering me? Signy never taught me how to manage darkness—only how to keep that kind of stuff out."

Viggo's thumb traced slow circles on my lower back. "Do you want to quit?"

"I can't leave Maja's sister in that camp. Or any of the other *älva*." I looped my hands around Viggo's waist. "Besides, she'll only help us find our senators if we help her free her sister."

"Yeah." Viggo sighed. "She's got us in a bad spot."

"Tell me about it," I muttered.

Viggo leaned back. He placed two fingers under my chin and pressed lightly, until I looked at him. "If you're truly uncomfortable, say the word and I'll fly us out of here. We'll find another way to free everyone."

"I'll be okay," I said. "I'll probably be better for it—having additional powers to tap into. It's just . . ."

"I get it," Viggo said softly. "What can I do?"

"Distract me. Make me forget about that awful energy and angry bees and your mean old cousin."

"Mmm." The pressure on my chin increased as Viggo brought my face to his. He pressed his lips against mine, leaving me lightheaded. "That help?"

"It's a start . . ."

I stood on tiptoe and kissed Viggo again. His hands framed my hips, tugging me against him as he ran his tongue along my bottom lip. All coherent thoughts fled my mind, and I slipped my fingers though his wavy strands, giving myself fully to the moment. Kissing Viggo, no matter where or when, was the single best distraction I could have asked for.

Or it would have been, if he hadn't pushed me away.

In Frigga's name, why?

"Everything okay?" I struggled to catch my breath.

"Everything's great." He glanced at the sky, now dotted with thousands of tiny points of light. "But if I remember correctly, you've given up a night of dancing to help our realm. Isn't the Solstice Dance happening right now?"

"Is it?" Viggo's kiss was still clouding my mind. "It's fine. I'm not that into dancing, anyway."

"Well, I am." Viggo placed my hand on his hip. He laced his fingers through the other, and brought it to his chest. "Humor me."

"Seriously, I'm not that great at—whoa."

I held tight to Viggo's hand as he dipped me over the grass. His eyes twinkled, and he swept me back in a slow arc.

"Where did you learn to dance?" I asked.

"There wasn't a lot to do on Svartalfheim. And apparently, my parents had a life before we got transferred there." He stepped lightly to one side, pulling me along with him. I stared at his feet moving in a small triangle, and struggled to keep up. "Just follow me."

"Easier said than done. Ouch!"

Viggo caught me as I stumbled on what must have

been a root. Or a hidden snake hole, if Alfheim had those.

Oh, gods, were there snakes in this meadow?

"You're trying to lead." Viggo increased the pressure on my lower spine, gently guiding me into place. "Relax."

"You relax," I muttered. But I eased the tension in my spine, and did my best to follow Viggo's footwork. It was hardly a thing of beauty, but at least I didn't trip on any more snake holes.

Seriously, are there snakes out here?

"So, I take it you didn't have any dances on Midgard." Viggo moved us closer to the tree.

"We had them," I said. "I didn't go."

"Why not?"

"In case you couldn't tell, dancing's really not my thing," I said. "Besides, Britney was head of the dance committee. I generally avoided being anywhere she was."

"How's she doing? I haven't seen her since the incident with Dragen."

"Better, apparently." I shuffled through Viggo's triangle-step. "Signy says her injuries should have healed enough that she can return to school next term."

"That's good, I guess. I hope her personality heals, too."

I nudged him with my fist. "You're terrible."

"I've heard worse." His chest rumbled against mine. "Huh. Would you look at that."

I glanced up, and followed his sightline. Across the meadow, tiny green flames flickered from the grass.

"My gods, is it on fire?" I whipped my head around, looking for something to extinguish the impending blaze.

Laughter rumbled in Viggo's throat. "Those are fireflies."

Fireflies?

"So, the meadow's not on fire?"

"No." Viggo's laughter deepened. "Weren't there fireflies on Midgard?"

"There were. Just not where I lived." I stared at the flickering light rising from the meadow. "You're sure that's what they are? Not flames?"

"Fire's not green, *Glitre.*"

"Maybe it is here. How should we know?" I blinked as a second wave rose from the grass. This time the lights seemed even brighter . . . and most definitely did not appear to have wings attached to them. *Gulp.* "Besides, if there are fireflies in Alfheim, wouldn't we have seen them before?"

"They're not native to our region." Viggo hadn't stopped his slow triangle steps. I had to whirl my head around to keep the apparently-not-fire in my sights.

"There!" A third wave ascended, this group close enough that I could practically touch them. "Jeez, they look exactly like fire."

"Hence the name. Sorry," Viggo apologized when my fist thumped his chest. "Here, let me show you."

He released his hold on me, and stepped toward the

lights. They blinked out, leaving him illuminated only by the moon and the stars. He stood very still, and after a minute the green lights flickered back on. They rose in lazy swirls, lifting from the meadow at a snail's pace. When a steady stream had formed around him, he slowly reached out and cupped his hands together. A faint, green light shone between his fingers.

"Here. Look." Viggo walked to my side. "This is a firefly."

I peeked at the gap between his fingers, and tried not to gape at what was most definitely not a green flame. A tiny, winged creature sat in his palm. Its hindquarters were illuminated like a lightbulb, emitting the faint glow I'd mistaken for fire.

"Whoa," I whispered. "I've never seen that before."

"Really? They're pretty common on Alfheim—and on some parts of Midgard too."

"Not in Granite Ridge." I studied the tiny creature, now flapping its wings so it hovered in Viggo's hands. "Is it okay in there?"

"I'll let it go. I just wanted you to see it first." Viggo opened his hands, and the firefly shot from his palm. It soared upward, joining the sea of green rising toward the tree. "Anything else I can teach you tonight? Dancing, fireflies . . . you name it."

I rolled my eyes at Viggo's laughter. "Glad I can amuse you."

"You do more than that." Viggo slid his arms around my waist, and pulled me close. "You inspire me. You never stop fighting to make our world a better place."

"I hope I don't let Maja down." My teeth worried my bottom lip. "I really don't know what I'm doing."

"You don't have to." Viggo stroked my cheek with one finger. "Just do your best—that's all anyone can ask of you. And remember—if it's too much, I'll evacuate you on the spot. No questions asked."

I craned my neck to press my lips to his jaw. "You're a good training partner. And an even better boyfriend."

"I do what I can." He bent and kissed me—a slow, lingering kiss that left liquid heat coursing through my veins. What little blood I had left in my head streamed due south.

Yum.

"Come on, *Glitre.*" Viggo's lips moved against mine as he spoke. "It's late—we'd better head inside."

"I'd rather stay out here." I shifted back into our kiss, losing myself in the ease of Viggo's arms. But much too quickly, he gently pushed me away.

Seriously?

"You've got a big day ahead," he reminded me. "And I've got to report in to Finna and catch her up to speed on the new plan. She was expecting us home tomorrow, but I'm guessing we'll be here another day."

"Probably." I sighed. "Assuming we free the *älva,* we'll still need time to track the senators. And figure out how to extract them, too. What if they aren't being concealed by clearing columns? What if it's some whole new energy I have to learn to fight and—"

"One day at a time," Viggo reminded me. "First, we

extract Maja's sister and the rest of the *älva*. That's the *only* thing you need to focus on."

"Right." I reluctantly released my hold on Viggo, and slipped my hand through his. We walked slowly across the meadow, careful not to step on any flickering, green lights.

As we entered the cave and made our way toward the corridor that housed our rooms, I glanced at the rows of closed doors. Maja had distinguished hers with a swirling pattern of purple, lavender and silver paints, and I blinked at the light spilling out from beneath it. The dark faerie was still awake, no doubt planning for the task we'd undertake in the morning. Knots built in my stomach as Viggo walked me past her room to our shared suite. My anxiety piqued after he left me at my bedroom door with one last goodnight kiss.

If I failed tomorrow—if I couldn't manage the darkness, or if I wasn't strong enough to break through the clearing columns that held the *älva*, then Maja's sister would remain trapped. And we'd have tipped our hand to whichever branch of Narrik's minions were holding her hostage, possibly alerting them to our bigger plan to free the senators and remove Narrik once and for all. And if they knew *that* was coming . . .

The knot tightened in my gut as I pictured everyone who was counting on me, from the prisoners to their families to the whole of Alfheim. I could do this. I *would* do this.

Or I wasn't fit to rule at all.

"ARE YOU READY?" MAJA stood in the middle of the meadow, her goth-chic ensemble a stark contrast to the morning's peaceful hues. Light peeked over the mountaintops, bathing the dewy green grass in a pinky-orange glow. The fireflies were long gone, replaced with winged creatures of a different variety.

Overnight, Rafe had amassed a veritable army of *älva*. They formed a protective circle around Maja, Viggo, and me, their intense faces forming masks of ferocity and their glowing weapons resembling tools of terror. I didn't want to think too hard about what they might do if the darkness overpowered one of us. It was why I'd asked Viggo to stay close—and if need be, pull me out of whatever I got myself into *before* Rafe's guards took me down.

"I'm ready." I fingered my new labradorite necklace as I turned to Viggo. "Is Signy set?"

I couldn't fathom how my aunt had managed to

arrange an attack team in less than eight hours. According to Viggo's earlier report, she'd wrangled most of Larkin's unit to help us . . . and half of another warrior's, too.

"Professor Bergen's team is in place," Viggo confirmed. "She has a full squadron moving into position as we speak. The ground assault will begin the moment you break the columns."

"Then I guess there's nothing left to wait for." I drew a breath. "Viggo, let them know we're moving in."

Viggo tapped his communicator. After a minute, he looked up. "Ground team's ready," he relayed.

I turned to Maja. "On your mark."

The dark faerie's kohl-lined eyes narrowed into thin slits. She widened her stance, squared her palms to the ground, and inhaled slowly through her nostrils. "Bring in the light," she ordered.

I snuck a glance at Viggo. His reassuring nod stilled a few of the butterflies beating against my belly button. With a slow breath, I closed my eyes. Then I mirrored Maja's stance, pressed my palms toward the grass, and pictured a stream beaming from the center of Alfheim straight through my feet. The light hit me with a jolt, and I stumbled backward as my entire body was filled with energy.

"Steady," Viggo said softly. His firm hand on my shoulder guided me into place, and I held my ground while a second wave coursed through my arms and down my torso.

When I was absolutely brimming with light, I called out to Maja. "I'm ready for the next set."

"Okay." Her voice was steely as she said, "Now bring in the dark."

With a new, considerably shakier breath, I raised my arms to the side. In an instant darkness swarmed around me, darting and weaving outside of my protective bubble as though it were searching for a way in. Pain wracked my body as the darkness dove, jabbing me with white-hot pricks like knives diving deep into my insides. There was so much—at least double the amount I'd felt last night. Had yesterday's bees told their friends I was now open for business? Gods, how many friends did they have?

Don't think about it, Aura. Just focus on the job.

Right.

Flexing my palm, I bent my fingers and opened a tiny hole in my protective sphere. The bees swarmed, pushing through the space and slamming into me with an intensity that knocked me backward. Viggo's hand returned to my spine, the familiar touch centering me enough that I reclaimed my balance. As darkness warred with light, I held my stance and waited for the surge to ebb. Pressure built atop my chest, choking me of oxygen and leaving with the disconcerting sensation of being towed under. My lungs expanded, but I couldn't sense the air enter my body. It was as if I was being suffocated from the inside. I inhaled deeper, harder, until a tiny stream pierced my chest. It traveled through me: a narrow, life-affirming passage that slowly expanded until I'd again mastered my breath. The bees, however, kept coming in strong. *Really* strong. After an eternity, I straightened my fingers, closing the hole and sealing off my space. The dueling energies swirled, ebbing and flowing until they merged into a singular, silvery mist. When I was confident I'd gained control, I called out to Maja. "I'm good."

"All right," she returned. "I'm sending you a scan. Let me know when it arrives."

Maja had explained that she worked in kind of a virtual reality setup—she'd project an image into both of our minds, and we were to direct our attack as if it were happening right in front of us. Our blasts would be transported across the realm to strike where needed, keeping us safe from physical harm and creating a stealthy assault that freed the *älva*.

Hopefully.

"Do you see it yet?" Maja asked.

"It's here," I confirmed as the image of a castle filled my mind. Its walls were transparent, allowing me a view of what appeared to be a live relay. Signy's team was already in place, her warriors positioned at each corner of the structure, and obscured within the castle walls. The prisoners were clustered in a small dormitory, with four guards standing just outside their door. A short corridor led to a large, open space. Based on Maja's descriptions, it must have been the work area. A quick perimeter scan revealed the four columns that arched into a dome.

"I see it," I confirmed. "It looks like they'll be on the move soon."

"We don't have much time. Focus on the front columns. I'll take the ones in the rear. Whoever clears first will help the other."

"Okay." I drew the silver mist into my hands and threw it outward. It struck the front pillars with a thunderous boom, its impact ricocheting across the distance and knocking me off-balance.

Viggo's arms slipped beneath mine as he helped me to my feet. "You okay?"

"I wasn't expecting that," I said honestly.

"What are you doing?" Maja yelled. "Go again."

I braced myself for a second hit and threw another surge at the columns. This time, the energy coming back at me was less intense—I managed to stay on upright long enough to send one of the pillars crumbling to the ground.

"I got one!" I cried.

"Don't start celebrating yet," Maja warned. "There are still three more—no, wait. Two more."

"Okay." I directed a series of pulses at the remaining front column. A small crack appeared in its base, but it remained mostly solid.

"How's. It. Coming?" Maja grunted.

"I'm not getting anywhere," I called out. "This one's stronger."

"When a stabilizer is deactivated, any surviving energy transfers," Maja yelled back. "It'll take more power to clear these two."

She was just sharing this now?

"Work together," Viggo ordered. "If the columns combined power, then you should, too."

"He's right." My arms trembled with the strain of sending another surge. "I'm not effective on my own. Move to the front pillar, and once it's down we can take on the rear."

"All right," Maja said. "Brace yourself."

My arms shook as Maja transferred her focus. A fierce wind whipped around me, whether nature or Maja-made, I couldn't quite tell. Her energy was much more powerful than mine—the jolt of her impact knocked me flat on my butt, and I scrambled to my feet, struggling to hold my own.

"Push harder, Aura!" Maja shouted. "It's breaking!"

"I'm trying," I gritted. I sent another surge at the pillar, and tried not to gape at the sizeable crack forming in its base. We were actually doing this!

"One. More. Time." Maja directed another wave at the column, and I did the same. The two streams collided at the base, and with a deafening crack the entire pillar crumbled to the ground. Dust rose from its remains, billowing in tiny puffs before being reabsorbed into the air.

"Now the back!" Maja ordered.

I regathered my composure and threw a series of pulses at the final column. It took longer than the third, and by the time we managed to down it, my arms wobbled and my legs shook. I'd never been more exhausted in my life . . . and I hadn't even lifted a sword.

Gods, I missed my *Verge* days.

"Ground team, move now. The columns are disabled." Viggo's voice from behind reminded me this was only half over. The rest of our team still had a job to do.

"Now what?" I panted.

"Now we wait for your aunt. Keep your guard up, and be prepared to strike anyone who—"

"Viggo, we need coverage on the left flank! They're too strong for our arrows, and we can't reach them in time!" Signy's normally calm tone was thick with tension.

"You hear her?" Viggo barked. "Left flank, cover . . . something!"

I refocused on the image inside my head. Two burly guards, stun-blades extended, moved in on the *älva*. The prisoners charged down the corridor, having apparently overpowered the first team of guards at their dormitory. Maja had said the *älva* were intuitive, but exactly how they'd realized the columns were gone, I did not know. Regardless, they now had a second, considerably scarier, threat bearing down on them.

"On it," I called. "Maja, I'll get the tall guy."

"I'll take his second."

We turned our streams on the guards. Maja flattened hers in one try, while mine managed to fight against the silvery mist I shot at him. His movements were noticeably slower as he continued along the hall.

But he was still strong enough to raise his spear to an *älva* as she flew past him. Electricity crackled from its tip, and he lunged at the faerie, pinning her to the wall and sending her into a fierce convulsion.

"Maja!" I screamed. "Help me take him out!"

"Gladly." Maja pulled back from her guard. She pushed her stream into mine, sending a surge so intense it threw the spear-holder with a burst of power. The aftershock thundered against the castle's stone walls, sending waves of debris raining onto the ground.

"They'd better evacuate," I warned. "Viggo, tell Signy the structure's unstable."

"On it." Viggo spoke into his communicator, and in my mental periphery I observed Signy's team making their adjustments. Those outside of the castle charged for the entrances, while those on the inside moved toward the remaining guards. They quickly disabled their opponents, then shifted their attention to evacuating the prisoners. They were nearly clear of the corridor when another crack rocked the castle. The building shifted on its foundation, and a fresh surge of rubble rained from its wall.

"Viggo!" I shouted. "Have Signy get everyone out of there! The western wall is coming down!"

"Signy, you need—"

"I know!" Signy's voice pierced the air. "But we can't clear the corridor. There are too many of us!"

"We have you." An unfamiliar voice rang through

the comm. When I shifted my attention to the scene inside my head, my jaw nearly unhinged.

What. The. Actual. Helheim?

The former prisoners had come together, making a circle around Signy's team. One by one they lifted the warriors from the ground, dodging rocks and rubble as they flew along the corridor and into the open space. With the columns eliminated, there was nothing keeping them in. The *älva* launched for the sky, carrying their charges well above the castle and flying toward the mountain. The second they'd cleared out, the structure came tumbling down. The castle caved in on itself in a heap of stone and dust and darkness.

Breath caught in my throat as I scanned the scene for any survivors. "Did Signy get out?"

"Professor Bergen, report in." Viggo spoke hurriedly into his comm.

"I'm clear." Signy's voice made my heart jolt. *Thank gods!* "And so is the rest of our team. The *älva* saved us."

"Everyone?" I squeaked.

"Everyone," she confirmed.

"What about Emilie?" Maja blurted. "Is my sister hurt?"

"Hold on." Signy's voice was muffled as she conferred with someone on the other end of the comm. "Emilie is fine. She carried Larkin out."

"Good." Maja's heavy exhale tugged at my heart. If it had been Elin, I'd have been sick with worry.

Thank gods.

"We're just touching down," Signy said. "Give us a minute to sort ourselves out. We can debrief in five."

Relief coursed through me and I dropped to the ground with an exhausted *oomph*. When I opened my eyes, Viggo knelt beside me, his face mirroring my own relief. Maja was doubled over a few feet away, breathing heavily. And Rafe's warriors remained in their circle, gratitude painted across their stoic faces.

We'd done it. We'd freed the *älva*. The only question that remained was . . . what was Narrik going to do to retaliate?

As it turned out, the answer to my question was complicated.

"Your senators were relocated." Maja looked up from a hologram. She, Viggo, Rafe, and I sat around a table in her family's living quarters, while her mother, Syrra, readied food in the kitchen. The Sorenssöns were eager to see Emilie, but they knew Signy and her team would be in touch as soon as they'd determined the best way to get everyone safely away from the capital. In the meantime Maja, true to her word, was focused on tracking our *Opprør*. The extraction itself would follow the same steps we'd used to free the *älva* . . . but now we had a different problem.

The senators weren't where we thought they'd be.

"*Skit.*" Viggo leaned forward to scrutinize the glowing, blue image hovering atop the table. "They were *just* there this morning."

"They were." Maja adjusted the band she wore around her head, and the hologram shifted to a wider frame. The device was something Maja had developed to project her mental images to a broader audience. According to Rafe, it had proven immeasurably valuable in helping his warriors protect their colony. I had no idea how it worked, but I was *definitely* talking to Maja about it when everything calmed down. We needed to know how to replicate that tech.

"See this room here?" Maja pointed to one of the open areas in what appeared to be a series of subterranean caverns. "This is where they were being held. But the trace on the heat signatures is faint enough to suggest they were evacuated four hours ago—not long after we freed my sister."

Viggo swore again. "Do heat signatures leave a trail? Is it possible to track where they went?"

"It is," Maja confirmed. "But remember, they've got blockers in place around their new cell, too. So, I can't say with certainty that they're being held here." Maja tapped her headband again, and the hologram pulled back to reveal a rotating model of a seaside cliff. She used two fingers to spin the model around, then raised her hands to the image, and drew them apart. The hologram zoomed in on a new series of tunnels, which led almost directly to the ocean. Maja pointed to the highest cavern—one nestled well above the sea. "But I can say it's highly likely."

I studied the image. "Are the blockers the same kind we dealt with this morning? Or have those changed, too?"

"See those wavy lines around the cavern?" Maja gestured. "That's how my mind views clearing columns. But there are jagged ones as well—the ones between the waves. I haven't seen anything like them before."

"Awesome." I exhaled heavily. "So, we have no idea what we're dealing with."

"Not entirely." Maja's mom set a plate of lefse on the table. Black braids swung over her shoulder as she slid into the chair beside her daughter. "Clearing columns are unnaturally strong—very few projections can maintain a charge in their presence. If those lines are a secondary block, they have to be emphyr walls."

"Great." Maja groaned. "Something I've never managed to cut through."

Viggo and I swapped worried looks. "What are emphyr walls?" he asked.

"A *super* dark blocker." Maja shook her head. "You thought the clearing columns were hard? Nobody's ever managed to break through these."

"I did once." Syrra looked at Rafe with a soft smile. "To get to you."

Rafe placed his hand atop his wife's. "Thank gods you did."

Maja's eyes widened. "Is that how your parents trapped you on Svartalfheim? Using emphyr walls?"

"Yes." Syrra turned to Viggo and me. "Let me

rewind a bit. I was born on the dark realm, but I left many years ago. From the time I was quite young, I made no secret of my distaste for my birth realm's . . . proclivities. After my first escape attempt, my mother and father set protections around our compound. I quickly learned to cut through their basal blockers, confounders, and most of the entry-level dark spells."

Maja's mom was no joke.

"After a while, the protections got more complicated. Thankfully, my parents were never fully aware of my capabilities."

"Or your indomitable determination," Rafe said proudly.

Syrra flushed. "When they conjured the emphyr walls, they were so sure I wouldn't be able to break through them they took a trip to Muspelheim. They were meeting with high-ranking fire giants when I managed my escape. I came straight here, and never returned."

Seriously? "You got into Alfheim? But how?"

"This was before the barrier," Syrra said gently. "Things were simpler then."

"Tell me about it," I muttered.

"So how did you do it?" Maja blinked at her mother. "How'd you break an emphyr?"

"I only managed it once, and it nearly killed me. But if I'd had your abilities—or yours, Aura . . ." Syrra studied each of us in turn. "Being of both realms gives each of you unique abilities. You're in a better position than I was to overpower their protections."

"Can you teach me?" Maja pressed.

"You're far more advanced than I ever was." Syrra's eyes sparkled with pride. "I have every confidence you can learn."

Viggo leaned forward. "Can she learn fast? If they've moved our senators once, they might do it again—and this time, somewhere even more remote. I'd rather we act before they get that chance."

Maja shot her cousin an irritated glare. "You think I'm a slow learner?"

"No." Viggo held up his hands. "I just—uh . . ."

"I'm kidding." Maja rolled her eyes.

I arched my brow at Viggo. I'd had no idea Maja could joke.

Who knew?

"I'll figure it out." Maja shrugged. "Mom and I will break through the blockers. You guys make sure you have a solid team on the ground."

"Can you see anything else?" I studied the holo-gram. "How many guards they have, what the best points of entry are . . . any insights that will help us?"

Maya tilted her head. She used her fingers to zoom in on the beach at the base of the mountain. "This should be the easiest entrance. It's unguarded at the moment—though my guess is they haven't had time to relocate yet. Moving that many prisoners probably took most of their resources, and staffing the exits would be a secondary priority."

"So, we'll go in there." I squinted at what appeared

to be a narrow opening in the cliff. "And follow . . . this tunnel here?"

"No. That one's wide. After today's breakout, they'll be expecting another. Unless they're stupid, they'll have guards on the ones that are large enough for an extraction team." Maja pointed to a narrower channel. "Use this one. You'll only be able to bring a few of your warriors in at a time, but it's small enough they may not think to watch it as closely."

"What about here?" Rafe tapped an entrance to the left of the cavern. "Could we fly in an *älva* team through this one?"

My heart warmed. "You're coming?"

"You saved our daughter." Rafe squeezed his wife's hand. "You will *always* have an ally in us."

"Always," Syrra repeated. "Our resources are yours."

"Thanks," I said softly. "That's going to make this a *lot* easier."

"We'll handle the air strike, and the blocker breakdown," Rafe said.

"And we'll take care of the ground team." Viggo turned to me. "When do you want to move?"

"We'll need to give Signy time to get the *älva* out of the capital, and regroup. And it'll probably take her team a full day to travel south—most of them can't fly." I wrung my fingers together. "Is two days too soon?"

"It may not be soon enough," Maja warned. "By then, your officials will probably have been moved again."

"Let's hope not." A loud rumble echoed from my stomach. My cheeks flamed in embarrassment. "Sorry."

"Eat." Syrra pushed the lefse plate to me. "All of you. Then, Maja, you and I have work to do."

Viggo turned to me. "And we need to figure out how we're going to up our weapon game." He tilted his head at his waist. "These daggers are the only things we brought."

"Show me." Rafe offered his palm. Viggo removed his blade from its holder, and passed it across the table. Rafe studied it for a moment, then looked up. "Is Aura's similarly made?"

"I think so." I handed Rafe my own dagger. His face illuminated as he took it in his other hand.

"I can enhance these," he said confidently. "In fact, if you come with me, I can show you some other weapons that may be of use. What do you usually work with?"

"What do you have?" Viggo practically salivated.

"Everything," Rafe said seriously. "What we weren't able to bring with us, we've either procured or crafted using our, erm, talents."

"The dust." Viggo glanced at me. "Do you think Aura and I will get that, too?"

I turned pleading eyes to Rafe. If he told me I was going to grow magic faerie dust that I could use on whatever I wanted, I was going to explode with happiness.

"You might." Rafe studied Viggo's wings. "There is a hereditary component, so even though it skipped your father it may still pass to you. Aura, did anyone in your family have that gift?"

"I don't know," I said honestly. "My grandmother doesn't have it. And my mom died when I was little, so I can't say."

"Hmm." Rafe pressed his lips together. "Well, you'll just have to see when your powers fully vest. Now grab some of that lefse and follow me. I'll show you our weapons vault."

"You have an entire vault?" Viggo's voice climbed several decibels. "Nice."

Rafe chuckled as he stood. "I have a feeling you're going to enjoy our stores nearly as much as I do. Come on."

Viggo and I each snagged some food and followed Rafe from his living room. As we walked, I shot a grateful look at Maja. Whatever else had passed between us, in this moment I was filled with gratitude. She was helping us track down our *Opprør*. And in doing that, she was working to create the Alfheim I wanted to be a part of.

I'd be forever grateful.

VIGGO AND I SPENT the two full days training with Rafe's warriors. We needed that much time to manage even a basic level of competence with the dust-enhanced weapons. Their blades projected energy bursts so strong, more often than not we found ourselves flat on our backs. It took half of a day before Viggo and I could wield them . . . and another half before we could send out a charge without draining ourselves. By the end of day one I was exhausted, sore, and mentally drained in ways I'd never been before. And at the end of the day two, my muscles trembled with a ferocity that gave me zero confidence in my ability to take down a single guard. But confidence didn't matter given the enormity of the dangers we faced. We had to push forward, whether we were ready or not.

Our world literally depended on it.

Signy had left the newly released *älva* under the

care of a *Protektor* unit. Now, she guided her recovery team into place near the beachside caves in the south. Rafe's unit would make the twelve-hour flight with us to the rendezvous point, then orchestrate an air strike while we moved in on the ground. Maja and Syrra would handle the dismantling of the blockers. They'd remain in the northern colony, protected by a small warrior unit, and let us know once they'd broken down the columns and walls. They'd also run remote surveillance, with Maja watching for additional dangers or further relocation attempts. We had a *lot* of pieces moving at once. I crossed my fingers that every-thing went according to plan.

Our flight took longer than expected owing to fierce winds, but eventually we reached the south. Rafe's warriors were the first to touch down. He instructed a small unit to land on the beach beside the cliff. They scoured the area for threats before giving us the all clear. My shoulders trembled with the strain of our long flight. The moment my feet hit the white sand, I dropped to my knees, careful not to cut my leg on my holstered sword. Viggo dropped in beside me, his stoic features bearing no sign of exhaustion. Instead, he held out a hand and pulled me up.

"We'd better move, *Glitre*. We're exposed."

"I'm aware." I jogged the short distance to the meeting point. Once there, I joined the huddle of *älva* tucked behind a rocky outcropping. "Where's Signy?"

"The ground team is half a mile away." Maja's voice came through my comm. "Move farther inside the cave

—if the captors have scanners, you'll be less detectable there."

I motioned at Viggo, who waved the group forward. "Everyone in."

"What if the other side has someone like you?" I spoke to my wrist. "They'll already know we're here."

"That's what the air team's for," Maja said. "There's a confounder in that unit—she uses her dust to impair awareness."

"Meaning?" Viggo came to stand beside me.

"Meaning if I see anyone start to move on you, I'll order the confounder to unleash her abilities."

I glanced nervously at Viggo. "What if we get caught in the dust? Won't we be, uh, confounded too?"

"The dust is coded," Maja explained. "It won't affect members of our party. Now get inside. There's a captor patrolling the far end of the beach. I'll reroute the ground team until he shifts position."

My comm beeped off, and I nervously followed Viggo into the cave.

"Hey." He tugged my bottom lip from between my teeth. "They'll be fine."

"Yeah . . ." I pulled my shoulders back. "I'll just feel better when I can see it for myself."

Viggo reached out to wrap his hand around mine.

A small eternity passed before Signy *finally* appeared at the cave's entrance. She walked toward us, her team trailing behind. She'd brought with her a small group of warriors, *Protektors*, and—

"Ondyr. Hey, man." Viggo released my hand to clap

his friend on the shoulders. "Nobody told us you and Zara were coming."

"Last-minute call." Ondyr nodded at my aunt. "Apparently, we were short on numbers. Professor Bergen said if we did well, we could skip combat next year."

"What I said was that you could earn extra credit for aiding the rescue efforts," Signy corrected. "All *Verge* classes remain mandatory."

Ondyr shrugged. "It was worth a try."

"Aura." Signy drew me in for a quick hug. "How are you holding up?"

"I'm fine," I said. "Glad we're on the homestretch."

"That's my girl." Signy squeezed my shoulder.

"You need to meet Rafe." I looked around, until I spotted Viggo's uncle. In a few steps I'd closed the distance between us, my aunt on my heels. "Signy, this is Rafe. He's Viggo's uncle, and commander of the Faerie Corps. Rafe, this is my aunt—one of Alfheim's *Protektors*, and leader of this ground unit."

"Good to meet you." Rafe bowed his head. "Aura's spoken very highly of you."

"And you as well." Signy smiled. "Thank you for standing with us."

"You freed my daughter. It is the least I can do." Rafe's eyes tugged downward. "How is she?"

"She's strong," Signy said admiringly. "She told me if you didn't have a unit available to escort them home, she'd lead her people herself. You raised an incredible girl."

"He raised two," I said. "You've got to meet Maja. She's difficult, no offense, but she's *really* smart. Definitely the energy warrior you want on your side."

"I heard that." Maja's dry voice came through the comm.

"I said no offense," I muttered.

"Move into position," Maja instructed. "The guards are heading around the far side of the cliff, which means you have a clear shot at the entrance to the smaller passage. Remember to stay to your left at the first three breakoffs. I'll send an image to your comms. Hold on . . ."

"It's through." Rafe waved with both hands, and his team gathered around. Zara moved into position at my side, and the rest of Signy's team circled up.

"Hey." I nudged Zara with my shoulder. "Thanks for doing this."

"You kidding?" She spoke out of the corner of her mouth. "I wouldn't have missed this for the world."

My heart tugged. As dark as Alfheim had become, we were lucky to be surrounded by friends who were willing to fight to bring back the light. Whether that fight took us an hour or a decade, there was a bright future awaiting us.

Right after we got out of this cave.

"Everyone knows their positions." Rafe raised his voice to address the group. "Siro and Vienna, bookend the ground team. The rest of my unit, follow me to the top of the cliff. We'll enter through the northern passage, and disable any guards between the prisoners and the exit. Signy." Rafe turned to my aunt. "My wife and daughter should have the blockers cleared by the time your team makes it up the tunnel. We'll meet at the cavern in approximately ten minutes. The prisoners will be extracted in twelve."

"I like that confidence." Signy clapped her hands. "Okay, ground team. You have your orders. Move out."

Two of the *älva* flew from the cluster. The male positioned himself at the entrance to the cave, while the female stood beside me.

"I'm Vienna." She raised her palm. "I'm taking the rear."

"I'm Aura. I'll be right ahead of you. Viggo, you've got the other glowy sword—you want to go to the front and protect Signy?"

"I doubt Professor Bergen needs my protection." Viggo winked. "But I'll head that way. Ondyr?"

"I'm staying with Aura. She's way tougher than you." Ondyr schooled his face into a mask of innocence.

"Fine. Zara?"

"I'll guard you, if that's what you're asking," Zara replied.

Viggo shook his head, and fell in behind Signy. We acted on her signal.

Icy wind swirled off the ocean, blasting my cheeks and whipping my braids against my face. The temperature had dropped considerably while we'd been in the cave, the lack of warmth enhanced by the rapidly setting sun. A smattering of stars had just begun to peek through the dusky sky, and while my mind appreciated the tactical advantage of entering the mountain in near-darkness, my body couldn't wait to get out of this cold.

Note to self: bring wind-jackets on missions.

"The point of entry is clear." Maja announced through my comm. Ahead, Viggo conveyed her message to Signy. The ten of us moved in a tight line, squeezing through a crack in the cliff wall and entering a narrow tunnel. It was barely wide enough for two of us to stand shoulder to shoulder, and I hoped we didn't run into any threats that required more than a dagger to defeat. No way could we swing a sword in this space.

We'd made it halfway up the mountain when a chill raced across my neck.

"Signy," I called. "Stop."

"What is it?" Since she'd rounded a corner, I couldn't see my aunt. But the tension in her voice let me know she was on alert.

"Someone's watching us. I can't tell if they're in front of us, or if—"

"Aura! Get down!" Vienna shoved me to the ground. I flattened myself against the stone as a burst of light flashed from behind. Vienna had sent some kind of blast along the tunnel, and it fired at whoever was observing our team. As I raised my head, I could barely make out the silhouette of a man. He looked to be around seven-feet tall, with broad shoulders and a blade that glinted in the light. Despite his recent hit, he staggered forward, closing the distance between us at an alarming pace. Whoever he was, he wasn't going away.

Vienna swore.

"I'll cover you." I pushed myself to a standing position. "Wait for my call then hit him again."

I squared my hips toward Vienna and drew a breath. Pulling strength from the mountain, I focused on the bubble surrounding me. I expanded it until it encompassed Vienna, too. Once she was secure, I drew another breath, held out my hands, and focused on the swirling light within my chest. It fizzed like the Italian sodas I'd loved back on Midgard, with tiny sparks pinging around between my ribs. It only took a second to corral the energy into two balls, and to send them through my arms, where they waited for launch.

"Now!" I called.

A second flash barreled along the tunnel. As it moved, I fired two white beams from my hands. The light laced with Vienna's, creating a near-blinding blast that knocked the blade-bearer off his feet. He hit the wall with a deafening crack. His spine bent unnaturally as he arched to the ground.

"Is there a second one?" I squinted at the tunnel.

"I can't tell," Vienna said. "Stay at the ready."

"Do you need an assist?" Signy yelled.

"Not sure yet," I called. "He's not moving, so I think this one's been debilitated, at least."

"Maja says we're clear," Viggo shouted from around the bend. "And she's sorry she didn't see him coming. She was working on the columns."

"That's where her focus needs to be," I said. "Tell her I'll scan from here on in. I'm not as good at it as she is, but I'll do my best."

Viggo must have relayed my message, because a few seconds later Maja's voice came through my comm.

"Sorry about that." She sounded frustrated. "Are you sure you can handle the scan?"

"We need you to get those blockers dissolved," I said. "I'll take care of things on this end."

"Thanks." Maja exhaled heavily. "Let me know if you change your mind."

I signed off, and turned to Vienna. "I'm going to check the mountain for other lifeforms. Watch my back? And be sure to tell me if you need me to switch gears."

"Of course." Vienna nodded.

"Should we hold our position?" Signy called from around the corner.

"Give me a minute." I retreated inward, then sent my attention along the corridor. Other than our would-be assailant, whose lack of pulse confirmed that he was no longer a threat, I didn't sense anyone between us and the beach. I redirected my focus forward, and double-checked before giving Signy the all clear.

"There's a bunch of them at the end of the tunnel," I warned. "But we're good until then."

"Keep me apprised," Signy called. "Siro, let's move."

Vienna's front-of-line counterpart must have followed the order. In no time we were jogging through the tunnel, making our way along the mountain. I kept my focus on the signatures that guarded the cavern ahead, occasionally withdrawing to check that we weren't being followed. After a few minutes, the narrowing walls forced us to slow our jog to a walk. Before long, we filed through an opening so tight that my wings brushed against the rocks. Something sharp jabbed at my spine, and I shimmied carefully until I'd cleared the space. On the other side was a small-ish room—one just big enough to hold our group, so long as we stood with our shoulders touching. Viggo was directly to my right, his hand resting firmly atop his now-glowing sword.

Wait. They were only supposed to glow when we were in danger. Which meant . . .

I sent my focus behind me. The tunnel was still clear, so I checked the other side of the thick, rock wall Signy stood in front of.

Crêpes.

"You're aware there are about twenty guards on the other side, right?" I whispered.

"I assumed as much," Signy said quietly. "We've nearly reached the cavern, which means we're about to face the guards who are holding our *Opprør*. We can expect them to be fierce warriors, energetic assassins, and more likely than not, completely averse to fighting fair. Be as aggressive as possible in your attack. I want you to take them out before they see us coming. Vienna and Siro, cover us as best you can. Do not hesitate to strike if you see a threat."

"We never do," Siro said solemnly.

Gulp.

The backside of my neck tingled, alerting me to a new danger. My stomach lurched as I scanned the other side of the wall.

"Something's approaching the opening," I whispered. "It's time."

"Ready positions," Signy ordered. "Aura, stay back—I don't want you on the front line."

"I can—"

"You're our regent," she said sternly. "Moira, take my flank."

A broad-shouldered warrior stepped forward.

"Move out!" Signy charged through the narrow opening in the wall. Moira followed, with Ondyr, Zara, Viggo, and the rest of the ground team close following suit. I lagged a few seconds behind, with Vienna on my heels. Before I slipped through the crack, I drew my sword. It glowed, a sparkling golden hue that illuminated the near-empty space.

"Be cautious," Vienna warned. "In combat, the charge from our weapons is more intense than what's emitted in training."

"How so?" I drew my dagger, so I held a blade in each hand. Beams of light shot between the two weapons. Pulses fired up each of my arms, rocking me off balance so I slammed against the wall. I drew a steadying breath, squared my shoulders, and reset my stance.

Yikes.

"Never mind. I figured it out."

"Get ready." Vienna raised her palms to the opening. "If our opponents are as strong as I sense them to be, we're in for the fight of our lives."

I swallowed hard.

Here we go.

"CLEAR THE ENTRY!" SIRO bellowed. I skirted quickly through the opening, careful to keep my back to the rocks. My gut seized as I scanned the cavern. Its walls stood a hundred-feet-high, with floor-to-ceiling energy barriers blocking the far quadrant of the room. The rest of the space was taken up by dozens of warriors fighting for control. Rafe's *älva* swooped from corner to corner, their glowing swords raining blasts on the sea of black hooded guards. Several of the winged warriors fought from the ground, lashing out with spears and daggers that somehow sent fiery beams into their opponents. Ahead of me, Signy drove her sword through a figure whose shoulders were easily twice the width of hers. To my right, Zara and Ondyr tag-teamed a guy who may well have been half-giant, while on my left—

"Aura! Down!"

I dropped to the dirt. A second later something

hard struck me from behind, forcing the air from my lungs on a *whoosh.* A heavy object rolled against my shoulder as the air filled with the stench of sulfur.

Yikes.

Viggo's legs came into view.

"Do I want to know what that is?" I asked. I lifted my head and he offered his hand.

"Nope. Just get that sword up and be ready for some kickback."

I shifted my sword and dagger to one hand, and let Viggo help me to my feet. Once I was steady, I transferred my dagger to my left hand and looked down. I tried not to gag at the newly severed head wobbling on the ground.

"Where are we needed?" I asked.

"Maja and Syrra still haven't gotten through the barriers." Viggo jutted his chin at the glowing columns in the corner of the room. "But once they do, the senators are going to require coverage."

"Got it." Movement from my right pulled my focus, and I quickly spun toward one of the hooded figures. When he charged at me, I drew my elbow back. As he passed I stepped to the side, driving my dagger between his ribs. He lunged. His hands wrapped around my neck as he fell. I wrenched my head, but his hold was too strong. My knees buckled and I dropped to the ground with him. Fire filled my lungs as he tightened his grip, and when he dug his thumbs into the hollow of my throat, pain exploded inside my head. I withdrew my dagger, fully intending to stab my way out of certain death. A flash from above forced my eyes closed, and it was only after the cloak of sulfur assaulted my gaping mouth that I dared open them again.

Viggo stood beside me. His sword dripped with my attacker's blood.

"These blades are no joke." His hand trembled slightly.

"You okay?" I quickly jumped to my feet.

"No worse than usual." He transferred his weapon to his other hand, and shook out his arm. "We'd better move."

"Already on it." I dodged a blast of *älva* fire and darted across the cavern. On the way, I managed to take out one of the smaller guards—it was death by impaling, a disturbingly easy defense with my highly charged sword. The fact that I'd just taken a life left my gut roiling, but I kept my focus forward and continued running. I'd nearly reached the glowing columns when someone cried out from behind.

"Arugh!"

Twenty feet away, Viggo fought off another impossibly large guard. Light pulsed from his sword as he swung it overhead. A *clang* echoed as Viggo's massive blade clashed with his opponent's considerably smaller one. The disparity didn't slow his attacker. Instead, the guard clutched his sword in one hand, and used the other to level Viggo in the gut.

I swore as Viggo doubled over. The guard raised his

arm, clearly intending to drive his sword through my boyfriend's back.

But I wasn't about to let Viggo die.

I threw my weapons to the ground and raised my palms. With a cry, I summoned beams so thick, my arms burned with the effort of forcing them out. Pain lapped at my skin as the energy made its way down my arms before ripping through my hands in two intense streams. When the light hit Viggo's attacker, he flew across the cavern. His head met the wall in a *crack* so fierce, it echoed throughout the cavern. As his body crumpled to the ground, I scooped up my weapons and raced to Viggo's side.

"That was close." I panted as I ushered him toward the relative calm of the columns. The guards seemed to be staying clear of the light. Whether they wanted to protect themselves from the blockers, or keep their captives isolated, I couldn't tell. Either way, it worked to my temporary advantage. "Are you okay?"

"Yeah." Viggo wiped his forehead with his arm. "Guess I owe you one."

"Let's both stay alive and call it even."

"Deal."

"Maja." I spoke into my comm. "Where are we on the columns?"

"Nearly there," she grunted. "The last column's the strongest."

"*Cover me?*" I mouthed to Viggo.

He moved in front of me and raised his sword. I quickly scanned the room, my heart leaping as I ran a headcount. Somehow, the odds had shifted slightly in our favor. Though the ground was littered with bodies, most were clad in the hooded garb of our opponents. And while the fight still raged around me, I was able to make out Signy, Ondyr, Zara, and Rafe, each holding their own against the massive guards. *Thank gods.*

Trusting that Viggo would look out for me, I turned away from the battle. I now faced the pillars holding our *Opprør* within their opaque walls.

"Okay." I raised my comm to my lips. "How do I help?"

"Mom and I already disabled the emphyrs, and the three columns adjacent to the cavern walls. See how those pillars are slightly dimmer?" Maja sounded tired.

"I do now." I narrowed my eyes at the lone free-standing column. "So, the one to my left is the target—that's the one we're taking down?"

"Yes. But there's a lot going on in that cavern," Maja warned. "You need to watch your back."

"That's Viggo's job. Gotta give him something to do."

"I heard that." The clang of metal on metal punctuated my partner's words. I glanced over my shoulder to find him driving a guard to the ground with his sword. The assailant fought hard, but Viggo delivered a swift front kick to the chest that knocked him down. He raised an arm, and Viggo quickly relieved him of his sword-hand.

Nice.

"You all right?" I called.

"Work fast, *Glitre*." Viggo turned to square off against another attacker.

With a nod, I focused my attention on the free-standing column. I opened my protections just enough to admit a handful of the angry bees, and I carefully blended them with the light that pinged around in my chest. Once I had the mixture under control, I pulled two balls into my palms and dropped into a fighting stance.

"Okay, Maja." I raised my fists to the column. "Talk me through this."

"The base is the weakest point," she said. "Direct everything you've got about three feet from the ground. Mom's going to hit the same spot from the back, and I'll come in from the side."

"Be careful, Aura." Syrra's melodic voice came through the comm. "If the pillar falls on you, its charge will be enough to knock you unconscious at best. And at worst . . ."

"Got it. Avoid the falling column." I tilted my head to my shoulder, eliciting a solid crack. "Say the word."

"Now!"

On Maja's command, I opened my hands. Energy shot through my palms, the full force of the blend striking the column so hard it shook. A sea of screams broke out inside the cell, and I hoped our efforts weren't hurting the senators. I withdrew slightly, angling my beams so they bore down on the column. Hopefully this would ensure any fallout would hit the ground . . . and not our *Opprør*.

"Give me more, Aura!" Maja called through the comm.

I gritted my teeth and focused on upping my attack. My arms trembled as another wave shot through them. "How's that?"

"It's too light," Maja shouted. "Go darker!"

Crêpes. My teeth clamped onto my bottom lip as I re-opened my bubble and let more darkness in. Black bees greedily swarmed the ball of light in my chest. They attacked from all sides, piercing its surface and sending white-hot shards ricocheting off my insides. I stumbled, shutting off the streams in my hands and clutching my chest to halt the pain. But the contact only made it worse—my fingers were like branding irons that burned through my skin. I dropped to my knees. The sensations were too intense to withstand.

"Aura!" Viggo's voice was muted—he sounded as if he were underwater. "Hold on, I'll be right—"

Clangs echoed through the chamber, the clash of swords resonating throughout the tension-filled space. A fresh jolt of pain rocked my chest. I balled my hands into fists and dug them into the ground. The room spun in a dizzying circle as I forced myself up. No matter how badly felt, I could not stop moving. Maja and Syrra needed me. The *Opprør* needed me. And, if the clanging from behind was any indication, Viggo could use an assist. *Fast.*

The room was a light-filled blur as I squared my shoulders to the column. I prayed the bees would behave before sending a jolt through my arms.

Gods willing, it wouldn't break me.

"Yes!" Maja's voice pierced my focus. "Whatever you're doing is working. Do you see that crack?"

At the moment, the only thing I registered was a carnival-like whirl that was fast giving me a migraine. But I'd take Maja's word for it.

"Do it again," she ordered.

It took everything I had to hold my control over the darkness inside of me. But I did as Maja instructed. Then I did it again. And again. For a seeming eternity, I shot beam after beam at the base of the column.

Boom!

The thunderous sound rocked the cavern. I hurriedly stepped aside as the column shifted, then leaned precariously forward. *We did it!* My heart leapt as the column wobbled. It was going to fall! Any second now it would . . .

Oh, gods.

Fear pierced my gut as I registered the pillar's trajectory. It was aligned with the spot where I'd just been standing. And directly behind me was—

"Viggo, look out!" I spun on one heel and sent a fresh beam at Viggo's attacker. He staggered backward, his blade falling from his hand as he tripped over a rock. I leapt toward Viggo. Pain pierced my shoulder as the bone connected with Viggo's hip. He exhaled loudly as I shoved him out of the column's path. We hit the ground hard, tumbling in a tangle of limbs and still-exposed blades. And though I distinctly felt each cut against my flesh, I kept us rolling for as long as I could. Gods willing, it was enough to clear the falling pillar. I had no intentions of dying in this cavern.

"Arugh!"

A surge of screams broke out as we slowed our roll. I turned my head right before the column crashed hard against the rocky ground. As it landed, it struck a cluster of guards, and the ensuing *boom* brought my hands to my ears. A jolt shot through the remains of the pillar, lighting the guards up like fireworks. Their cloaks burst into flames and their spines arched in what looked to be utter agony. No sooner had they crumbled into smoking heaps than the entire cavern was filled with the sulfurous odor I'd come to associate with their death. If their scent was any indication, Was there any way they might be from . . .

Had someone made a literal deal with Hel?

Gods, what exactly are we dealing with?

"Aura, the senators!" Viggo leapt to his feet, and I scrambled to do the same. I followed his eyeline to the corner of the cavern, where the remaining three pillars wobbled from left to right. "We have to make sure they don't touch the columns!"

"On it." I nudged the darkness from my chest, ignoring the burn as the bees resisted eviction. With shaky breaths, I drained the energy into the ground. Once it was clear I pressed against the boundary of my protection, growing it until it encompassed the now exposed senators. Terror emanated from their trembling hands and tightly shut eyes. One wrong move, and they'd fry just like the guards.

"Don't move!" I shouted. "Whatever happens, do not step outside of—"

"Oh, gods! It's falling!" One of the senators leapt from the huddle, charging away from the crumbling column.

"No!" I tried to expand my shield. But a piece of the pillar fell across the senator's path. She arched her back as she burned, the fire zipping along her threadbare robes. While I struggled to protect her cluster of colleagues, she fell to the ground. Flames lapped at her remains.

"Stay. There." I gritted to the survivors. "I've got you."

The remaining senators only nodded in agreement.

Crackles echoed across the cavern as the rest of the columns crumbled, then toppled over. The edge of my shield burned as pieces of the pillars bounced off of it—hot coals against a too-thin membrane. But the senators remained untouched, and when the final piece landed, I shakily withdrew my protection. I held out my hands as I approached the trembling *Opprør*.

"You're okay," I said slowly. "I'm Aura, and this is Viggo. We're here to help you."

"They're . . . dead," a tall man whispered. "All of them."

I turned around. In place of chaos stood a scene of quiet destruction. Signy's team was scattered across the cavern, some doubled over while others picked themselves off the floor. Rafe's warriors were alighting from their airborne positions. And a small cluster of *älva* stood in a circle, weapons drawn.

What was going on?

Viggo stepped beside me. "When the columns fell, so did the rest of the guards. All but one."

I followed his eyeline to the single survivor. A hooded figure stood defiantly in the circle of faeries. His face was covered, but his drawn shoulders and fisted hands let me know he wasn't about to go down easily.

Good thing a half-dozen *älva* had him at blade-point.

Rafe pushed through his team to stand in front of the man. He was shorter than the rest of his guards, and appeared to wear his cloak on a slightly smaller frame. Rafe pointed to the far wall, where a large black hole now swirled within the cavern. "I presume you entered through that?"

My heart clenched. I'd seen that hole before. With the sparks flying off its edge, it looked exactly like the one Dragen had come through when he'd entered from . . .

Oh, gods. The sulfurous odor suddenly made sense. Viggo had told me that Svartalfheim always smelled of rotten eggs. If the guards we'd killed had been from the dark realm, it could only mean that their leader was . . .

No.

"That can't be Dragen." I stepped closer to Viggo. "We sent him to Helheim. I saw it."

Signy stormed across the cavern, her sword pointed

at the still-hooded man. "Who are you? And how did you summon a portal?"

The man said nothing, simply drew his shoulders farther back and lifted his chin. His hood slipped slightly with the movement, and as the fabric rode up, I could have sworn I made out the boxy jaw and too-thin lips of—

"Narrik!" Signy hissed. "It's *you*."

Crêpes.

Before Rafe could react, Narrik drew a blade from his cloak. He drove the dagger into one of the *älva*, forcing her to double over. As she clutched at her stomach, he jammed his knee into her face. The contact elicited a sickening crack, and the woman soared backwards. Narrik dove for the portal, slipping into the blackness before Rafe's guards could seize him. The hole sparked, spun, and closed in on itself, sealing Narrik in whatever corner of the cosmos housed cowards.

Rafe swore loudly. "Follow him!"

"We can't." Signy shook her head. "And I doubt we'd want to be wherever he's gone. I'm sure there are more guards waiting for him. We need to move the prisoners to a secure location before he opens another portal."

"Maja?" I addressed my comm. "Which exit is the safest?"

"The upper," she said quickly. "It's closest, and leads to the cliff top, which will make for an easy extraction site. Have my dad's warriors fly the prisoners back to your base."

"Everybody hear that?" Signy clapped her hands together. "Rafe, do you remember where our academy is?"

"One never forgets," he said.

"Good. A *Protektor* team is guarding the *älva* in the *Verge* facility—it was the most secure place for us to take your citizens. Have your team fly the senators there. We'll follow on foot. Aura, lead them out."

"On it." I turned to face the still shell-shocked politicians. "Come with me. Quickly."

I waved them forward, directing Viggo to cover the rear of their line. Several of the *älva* flanked us as we made our way through the cavern. By the time we cleared out of the mountain, the sky was almost completely black. The only light came from a cloud-covered moon.

It only took a few minutes to assign each senator to an *älva*. And though each of them clung to their extractor in what seemed to be genuine terror, they allowed the faeries to fly them off the mountain. As they crossed the sky, the remaining warriors gathered around Signy. Zara and Ondyr stepped beside me, and I hurriedly scanned them for injuries. Zara's arm was bleeding, and there was a nasty slice across Ondyr's thigh. But they were both standing, and by some miracle, still in one piece. I'd take whatever I could get.

"The fastest route home is across the cliffs." Signy pointed to the rocky terrain that bordered the sea. "Keep a steady pace, and watch for unexpected portals. Aura, Viggo, we'll reconvene with you at the academy."

"No way." I shook my head. "Somebody's got to cover you from the air."

"It's too dangerous to be this exposed. Frigga only knows when Narrik might show up again—or how many guards he'll bring with him when he returns."

"Exactly." Viggo stepped forward. "We've got you from the sky. Just make sure everyone travels home safely."

Signy shook her head, but led her team across the cliff. She seemed tired, worn, and in all likelihood, was completely exhausted from the threat we'd faced. But she held her chin high and moved as the commander she was. I hoped one day, I'd be able to lead with her grace.

Viggo slipped his hand through mine, and squeezed lightly. "Ready to fly, faerie princess?"

I shot him a look. "That's faerie *warrior* princess, thank you very much."

"Whatever you say, *Glitre*." Viggo winked.

With a grin, I spread my wings and launched into the sky. Whatever obstacles lay ahead, Viggo and I were going to conquer them together.

Even if I had no idea how.

CHAPTER 18

THE NEXT FEW DAYS where a whirl of activity. By the time we made it to the academy, the senators had been debriefed and sent home to their families. They'd left the mountain malnourished, weak, and undeniably traumatized. But they were alive, thank gods. In time, they'd find their way back to their former lives. The once captive *älva* were reunited with their families, too. Though I'd been with the ground team, I'd heard that Rafe had wept when he'd spotted Emilie. According to Finna, he'd swept his daughter into his arms, loosened his hold just long enough to assess that Emilie was, in fact, okay, then hugged her even tighter than the first time. When he told her how much he loved her, Rafe's words had been broken up by his shoulder-heaving sobs. The reunion had been so sweet that most who had witnessed it had burst into happy tears.

Less happy was the discovery of Narrik's role in the

älva's detention. We learned that he'd been highly involved in their captivity, paying weekly visits to their camp and personally managing their living conditions. According to witnesses, he'd instructed the *älva* be kept in quarters poor enough to strip them of hope, but not abysmal enough to affect their dust supply. Narrik had ordered the dust harvesting, employing high-ranking military *Elementär* to siphon the magic from the faerie's wings before allocating it to the resources Narrik deemed most worthy. Some had gone to the barrier, but a portion had also been given to a *Styra*-led team who used the dust to control key government officials . . . including Queen Constance.

Apparently with certain manipulations, *älva* dust could be utilized as a mind-altering substance—an odorless, traceless drug not unlike those derived from Midgardian nightshade plants. Emilie had overheard one of the *Styra* tell Narrik to administer the powder on the rim of a glass, or mixed into a drink—it didn't sound as though his victims had been aware they were being compromised. Though my grandmother had known Narrik held *something* over her—something big enough for her to fear him. Now that both Narrik and his substance of choice were gone, I hoped some of Constance's fear would go away. She was finally free of Narrik's control . . . and we'd find out what kind of ruler she truly wanted to be.

"Let me get this straight." Finna looked up from a single sheet of paper. On it, she'd compiled the key points of the senator's debriefings. Now she, Viggo,

Elin, Ondyr, Zara, Wynter, Jande, and I sat around Signy's living room, discussing its contents over the bevy of baked goods my aunt had prepared between debriefing the *Opprør* and rehabilitating the *älva*. "On the night the senators were abducted, a team of hooded figures broke into the senate building. And *nobody* thought that was suspicious?"

"Nobody noticed, because they unleashed a gas that knocked most of the building's occupants unconscious." Jande wrapped his hands around a mug of tea. "The transcript I read said the entire building was offline for ten minutes—even the imaging feeds went down. The perpetrators must have drugged the security team and cut the connections."

"Obviously, security will need to be reevaluated," Viggo said. "A secondary, *uncompromisable* system should be implemented. Ondyr?"

"On it." Ondyr cracked his knuckles with a smile. "We had a few in play on Svartalfheim. I'm sure I can adapt one of them."

"What happened after the gas was administered?" Wynter picked at the edge of a chocolate cookie.

"Most of the senators were completely unconscious, but a few remember being blindfolded, dragged through the hallways, and stuffed into a transport." Finna glanced at the paper. "They were taken to a small, dark room—most likely the first of the prison cells inside the southern mountain. Two escape attempts led to the installations of energy columns.

The guards were determined to keep the senators incarcerated."

"The columns did their job," Zara growled. "The report I read said there was an altercation between a senator and a guard. Apparently at the end of it, the guard threw the senator into one of the columns. She died instantly, and the guard left her corpse in the cell —a reminder of what happened to those who challenged authority."

Viggo grimaced. "I hope he was one of the ones I killed."

"I'm just glad it's over," Wynter said sadly. "Those poor senators."

"I can't believe Narrik was behind their disappearance the whole time." Finna shook her head.

"We'd always assumed as much. But we weren't able to gather any evidence against him . . . until now." Signy carried a fresh plate of lefse from the kitchen to the table.

"What tipped his hand?" I asked.

"It was Emilie." Signy slid into a chair. "Her statement led us to the *Styra* and *Elementär* who were working with Narrik. Larkin interrogated them pretty thoroughly—by which I mean strong threats were issued."

"That sounds like Mom," Elin said dryly.

Signy smiled. "They broke fairly quickly. Apparently Narrik bragged to them about possessing something that would cement his role as Alfheim's true leader."

"The missing senators?" Elin guessed.

"Correct." Signy nodded. "He intended to do to the senators what he did to the *älva*—keep them healthy enough to stay alive, but in conditions that stifled their spirits. He figured at some point, once the realm grew truly desperate, he would offer a trade: the return of the senators, in exchange for his being named ruler."

"Is that why he drugged the queen?" Viggo asked. "So he could make sure she lost the trust of her people?"

"Yes," Wynter said. She pushed the plate of cookies across the table toward Viggo and Ondyr. They eagerly dug in. "I can't believe the regent could be so easily—and thoroughly— compromised. Aura, we're going to need to put checks in place to make sure that never happens to you."

"Seriously," I said.

"It's definitely troubling," Signy agreed. "But even more worrisome is Narrik's apparent alliance with a dark realm—one that supplied him with guards, and offers him the opportunity to travel by portal."

"He has to be in Svartalfheim." Ondyr took a savage bite of his cookie. "The Kyan Flats are crawling with sulfur—and the dark elves who live there are massive, just like those guards."

I drummed my fingers on the table. "You don't think Dragen escaped, do you?"

"It's *highly* improbable." Wynter shook her head. "We sent him to Hel's inner chamber. Nobody's ever come out of there alive. Though the occasional deceased makes their way to the Cloak."

I shuddered. "Who else could he be working with?"

"Literally anyone." Ondyr paused mid-bite. "Narrik is—or was—a powerful government officer. Any number of Svartalfheim's senators would have traded their fortunes to gain access to the light realm."

"Don't forget the fire giants," Jande said. "If Narrik could be bought, I'm sure leaders on Muspelheim would have thrown in bids."

"And Jotunheim," Zara added. "The frost giants have been trying to get control of Alfheim for years."

"So we have plenty of enemies. And apparently, so does Vanaheim. I talked to Idris yesterday—there haven't been any more breaches, but they still don't know who managed to get into their realm. Or how." I sighed. "What do we do now?"

"Well . . ." Finna and Elin exchanged a glance.

"I recognize that look. You're up to something." My eyes narrowed. "Out with it."

"Okay." Finna squirmed in her seat. "Remember before you left, when you told us to work out a proposal you could pitch to the senate? The one about reinstating the restoration teams, so we could fix the regions that died, and bring the whole of Alfhiem back to at least a semi-habitable state?"

"Yes . . . why?"

"Well, we did it!" Elin blurted. "We combed through old resolutions, followed the proper format, found precedents, and developed a cost-saving plan that even the most stubborn senators won't be able to find fault in."

My hand went to my chest. "You did all of that? When?"

"We took shifts," Jande said. "We realized we only needed two of us on ground ops at any given time, so during off periods we researched and wrote. We brainstormed the actual implementation during slow times so all three of us could work together."

"It's in our dorm," Finna said. "We'll walk you through it after we all get some rest."

"That's incredible." I blinked the moisture from my eyes. "I can't believe you did that on top of everything else you were dealing with."

"You asked us to help the realm," Elin said simply. "We weren't going to let you down."

My heart felt like it might burst from my chest. Thank gods for my friends. They were truly the greatest beings in all the realms.

"Hey. Don't cry." Elin reached over to pat my shoulder.

"I'm so grateful for you guys. For *everything* you've done for me, and for Alfheim, and for . . ." I sniffled. "Stupid tears."

"We love you too," Finna said easily.

I wiped my nose on my sleeve. "I can't wait to read your resolution. And propose this at the next senate session. And then . . ."

"And then we'll do we've always done." Viggo's fingertips brushed mine, and I looked over at him. His emerald eyes sparked with determination. "We implement change where we can. We eliminate darkness wherever it's found. And we wake up every day, determined to leave our world better than it was yesterday."

"Easy as that, huh?" I turned my palm so I could lace my fingers through his.

"Easy as that."

For all of our sakes, I hoped he was right.

A month later, I stood in the formal senate chamber. My argument was bulletproof, my speech impeccably rehearsed, and at Vendya's insistence, I wore my great-grandmother's power tiara atop my uncomfortably tight updo. The tiara's sky-blue crystals were meant to channel strength and wisdom, and, as Vendya pointed out, they coordinated with the navy pantsuit she'd designed for the session.

Some things never changed.

Most importantly, I finally faced a full senate—one made of both *Kongelig* and *Opprør*, all listening while I laid out the details of my friends' newly drafted Restoration Resolution. It provided not only the scientific and energetic blueprints for restoring Alfheim to its once vibrant state, but a promise to never again abuse the powers of its residents. Further, it fleshed out consequences so severe, no sound-minded individual would dare breach its parameters. As for those of unsound mind . . . if they ever returned, we'd deal with them. *Harshly.*

"And so." My fingers gripped the podium as I finished my statement. "I hereby request this governing body approve the Restoration Resolution in its entirety for the greater good of Alfheim, for our citizens, and for the realms we are sworn to serve."

Applause rocked the back of the chamber, the burst of noise erupting from silence. Heat crept along my neck as I glanced at the viewing gallery where my friends sat watching the vote. Maja raised one fist in solidarity, and Jande flashed me a grin that stretched from ear to ear. Near the side door, Signy and Larkin both beamed their approval. I willed the heat to drain from my cheeks as I scanned the rows of senators.

"I move we take this matter to a vote." Our newly appointed minister of state rose from her seat. In Narrik's absence we'd appointed Ella Andriskog, one of the returned *Opprør,* to serve in his former post. Ella was a seasoned senator, and someone we knew would lead fairly—*without* manipulating the crown.

"All those in favor of approving the Crown Princess's resolution, vote *ja.*"

The right half of the room immediately raised their hands to their data pads. I'd expected the *Opprør* to vote in my favor, but my throat tightened as my gaze shifted to the left. Several of the *Kongelig* pressed their fingertips to their data pads. When they'd finished typing, they looked at me and offered tentative smiles.

Holy. Freaking. Gods.

I glanced to the throne behind me, where Constance nodded regally.

"And all those opposed," Ella called.

The rest of the *Kongelig* typed furiously.

Ella's cherubic face lit up as she examined her data pad. "The *jas* have it. The Restoration Resolution is hereby passed."

A wolf whistle pierced the air. At the back of the room Maja stood on top of her bench, two fingers in her mouth and a fist in the air. Elin whooped enthusiastically beside her. And Viggo applauded at end of the row, his face fierce with pride. His eyes locked on mine and a wave of relief coursed between us.

We'd done it. We'd taken the first step toward reversing the nightmare Narrik had inflicted on our realm. Our work was just beginning, but we could be proud of what we'd accomplished. Our senators were home. Our home was on the road to recovery. And we'd ensured that no resident of Alfheim would ever again be exploited.

I shot Viggo a wink as I stepped down from the podium and shook Ella's hand. Once she dismissed the session, I crossed to Constance.

"You did well." She squeezed my hand. Before I could thank her, she'd escaped through the back door. My grandmother had been quiet since we'd briefed her on the extent of Narrik's wrongdoing. Whether she was disappointed or embarrassed, or something else entirely, I couldn't quite tell. For now, I'd decided to give her space. She needed time to lick her wounds before we began restructuring our cabinet. With the *Opprør* home, we were *finally* going to be able to bring in the representatives we needed.

Thank gods.

The senate floor buzzed with excitement for a good few minutes after Constance's departure. There were countless congratulations, and endless exclamations of relief. When the politicians began trickling from the room, Signy and Larkin came over to wrap me in tight hugs.

"Sweet girl," Signy whispered. "I am so proud of you."

"That makes two of us," Larkin seconded.

"Thank you. For *everything*." I squeezed them fiercely.

"Come on." Signy pulled away. "Your friends want to celebrate with you."

"The extremely subtle ones, over there?" I pointed to the rear of the chamber, where Finna bounced on her toes and Jande waved enthusiastically.

"Those are the ones." Signy led me in their direction.

When we reached the benches, Elin immediately threw her arms around me. "We did it!"

"Now we can get to work," Zara added. "My parents are visiting next week. They were on a restoration team in their day, and they'd love to brainstorm strategies with the new units."

"We'd be lucky to have them," I said honestly.

"Thank you. All of you. For everything you've done . . . and everything I'm about to ask you to do."

"Thank *you*, Aura." Rafe clasped his hands together. "You helped bring my daughter and the rest of our citizens home. You were brave to help Maja. And even braver to stand up to all of this." His gaze swept the now-empty chamber.

"I had a little help." I smiled at my friends. "And a *lot* of painful training."

"If you're talking about learning to manage dark energy, you're welcome." Maja pointed to the labradorite necklace I still wore. "You're going to need that again. Just you wait."

"Gods, I hope not." I shuddered. "I'm still recovering from last time."

"Tell me about it," Maja said wryly. "At least it's over. For now."

"Maja," Rafe acknowledged. "Let Aura celebrate. Today marks a big victory."

"And tomorrow begins her whole new level of workaholic-ness." Elin sighed. "But we'll be right there in the trenches with you. I promise."

"You always are." I shot my bestie a grateful grin.

"What do you say, *Glitre*?" Viggo's pride permeated the entire room. "Can we take a few hours off to celebrate?"

"I guess," I said. "What did you guys have in mind?"

Signy's eyes darted to Viggo. "We *may* have set up a little thing in the academy courtyard. It's only a few desserts, and balloons, and . . . well, you'll see."

I arched my brow. "How did you know the resolution would pass?"

"Maja told us it would." Wynter pointed to Viggo's cousin.

"Maja," Rafe admonished. "You're not supposed to look into the future."

Whoa. Maja can do what?

I studied the dark faerie through narrowed eyes. "Hey, Maja?"

"Mmm?"

"Any chance you want to work with the government? Join the regent's cabinet, maybe?"

Maja tilted her head. "Do you want to know your future?"

"Me? Gods, no." I slid my arm around Viggo's waist. "I know everything I need to—for now, anyway. But since there's a crazy dictator with a grudge out there, well . . . we could use every bit of help we can get to keep things running smooth around here. Right?"

Maja pressed her lips together. "I'll think about it."

I looked at Viggo. "Honestly, that's a better answer than I'd expected."

Maja jutted her hip. "I *am* a team player, you know. Just ask Dad."

"I know you are," I said seriously. "That's why I want you on *my* team."

Maja shrugged. "Who doesn't?"

I grinned. "Maybe Signy's award-winning scones can convince you. Did you make any for this 'little event,' Signy? Perhaps those ones with the thick sugar granules on top?"

Signy folded her arms. "Do I *look* like this is my first garden party?"

With a laugh, we followed her out of the senate building, and made the journey back to Alfheim Academy.

True to form, my aunt had pulled together an elaborate spread. Long, linen-clad tables framed the courtyard. They were laden with every imaginable dessert, beverage, and of course, an endless supply of fresh blooms. Elin had strung tiny lights and streamers around the courtyard, and I had no doubt Jande and Finna were responsible for the bevy of crystals placed strategically around the party.

"For harmony," Jande called as I bent to study a purple stone that stood three feet tall. "We knew you'd want to jump right into work, so we borrowed some crystals to charge the space with restful energy."

"Are you allowed to do that?" I asked him.

Jande shrugged. "The faculty's on summer vacation, too. What they don't know won't hurt them. Right?"

"I guess not." I laughed as I let him drag me over to the cake table. He shoved a plate filled with scones and waffles in my hands before stuffing an entire cupcake in his mouth.

"What?" He grinned through a mouthful of crumbs. "It's a party."

And it was. We spent the rest of the day celebrating. Rafe, Signy, and Larkin entertained us with stories from their days at the academy, while Maja and Wynter swapped stories about their unconventional gifts. If Maja did decide to work with us, I had no doubt she and Wynter would become fast friends.

At some point, Elin turned on the music, and Jande challenged everyone to a dance-off. Zara impressed us with her hip-hop moves, but Rafe proved to be the biggest surprise of all. He waltzed an embarrassed Maja across the grass in a graceful display of athleticism. When they'd finished, Jande demanded he stick around to teach a ballroom class at the academy.

"Please? Please, please, puh-lease?" Jande folded his hands together. "Ondyr can learn so much from you."

"Hey," Ondyr objected. "I dance just fine, thank you."

"You do many things well," Zara said solemnly. "Dancing is not one of them."

Ondyr growled at his training partner.

Viggo nudged my shoulder with a smile. "I'll sign up if you do."

I gazed at him. "Guess your parents weren't the only Sorenssöns who had that particular gift, huh?"

"I guess not." Viggo snaked his arm around my waist and tugged me closer. He lowered his head, and pressed his lips to mine in a slow kiss. A pulse of heat shot straight through me as the pressure of his lips increased. I sighed contentedly as Viggo ran his tongue along my bottom lip and hiked my hips against his. My heart thundered, the intensity of Viggo's kiss overwhelming me in the best possible way. When Viggo finally pulled back, my head spun from the lack of oxygen.

"Mmm." I murmured. "What was that for?"

"For being you." Viggo kissed me again. My wings fluttered, and he reached out to tweak the tip of one. My sword tattoo sparkled in the late-afternoon sunlight, the mate-mark a perfect match to the one on Viggo's wing. "Lucky thing, the Norns pairing us up."

"We're *very* lucky." I rested my head on his chest, feeling the gentle rhythm of his heartbeat against my cheek. "For a lot of things."

And we were. As Viggo slipped his arms around my waist and held me close, Elin turned up the music. Viggo rubbed lightly at the small of my back as we swayed to the beat. I angled my head to kiss him lightly before settling into his easy rhythm. While we danced, I took in all of the happiness that surrounded us. Rafe and Maja walked Ondyr through a basic waltz, while Jande and Zara struggled to contain their laughter. Finna, Wynter, and Elin twirled beneath a string of lights, while Signy and Larkin chatted over a plate of scones. My heart swelled as I took in the sight of everyone I loved best, relishing an evening of pure happiness. In this moment I felt joy, love, and complete and total peace.

Not long ago, I'd pledged to protect Alfheim from forces that seemed insurmountable. I'd vowed to ensure our realm remained a sanctuary—one where everyone was safe to be exactly who they were, whether that was a senator or an *älva* or a student who just wanted to leave our realm a bit better than it had been when they'd found it. But I'd quickly learned I wasn't meant to do any of that alone. I was going to protect our realm with my friends at my side.

It was time for us to get to work.

ACKNOWLEDGMENTS

As always, I owe endless gratitude to my adventurous family—I am so grateful that God gave me you! Thanks to my longtime editor, Lauren Clarke, and the lovely Anna of CREATING ink. Thank you, Alison, for your brilliant insights and thoughtful feedback, always. *Takk* to my lovely beta readers, Laura and Lorna, and to Mariana, whose endless patience keeps this Viking ship on course. And a huge thanks to the readers who have supported these Norse stories from day one—I couldn't do this without you!

And *tusen takk* to MorMorMa. Always.

ABOUT THE AUTHOR

Before finding domestic bliss in suburbia, internation-ally bestselling author S.T. Bende lived in Manhattan Beach (became overly fond of Peet's Coffee) and Europe…where she became overly fond of McVitie's cookies. Her love of Scandinavian culture and a very patient Norwegian teacher inspired her YA Norse fantasy books. And her love of a galaxy far, far away inspired her to write children's books for Star Wars. She hopes her characters make you smile, and she dreams of skiing on Jotunheim and Hoth.

Learn more about the world of S.T. Bende at www.stbende.com.

Aura's adventures continue in...
ALFHEIM ACADEMY: ROYAL REBEL

Aura Nilssen's life hasn't gone at all according to plan. She's the unwitting heir to a tainted throne, the recipient of not one but *two* unwanted legacies, and she's on the hit list of every dark realm in the cosmos. But with weeks to go before her graduation from Alfheim Academy and official coronation as queen, the reluctant royal thinks she can finally take a breath.

She should have known better.

When her allies' borders are breached, Aura knows it's only a matter of time before Alfheim is attacked. As dark powers move against her home, Aura and her friends set out to determine exactly who might be strong enough to overpower the light realms. With more than just Alfheim's future on the line, Aura will risk everything to save the world she's grown to love . . . and the warrior who's claimed her heart.

*Erik held me until my shoulders stopped shaking—whether it
was a minute or an hour, I couldn't tell. The only things I
knew for sure were:*

1. *I was trapped a thousand years in the past, with
   little hope of ever going home. And,*
2. *I was wrapped in the arms of the most absurdly
   gorgeous Viking to have ever walked the face of
   the Earth.*

Maybe my old life was overrated.

When seventeen-year-old Saga Skånstad discovers an

antique dagger, she's instantly sucked into a world where Vikings rule the seas and dragons roam the skies, and the only thing more dangerous than the chief who takes her captive is the rival who steals her away. The heir of Norway's most feared tribe is fierce, cold, and absolutely unyielding. With intruders encroaching upon his borders, Erik Halvarsson has little patience for the girl whose ignorance threatens his very existence. He enlists Saga in the magical Valkyris Academy, where she learns the skills she'll need to protect herself from foreign raiders and domestic terrors. But nothing can protect her from falling for the one guy in all the world she's absolutely forbidden to choose . . . or from risking everything to unlock the secrets that haunt him.

When darkness threatens Saga's new home, she must decide whether to return to the life she's always known, or fight for a love she never could have imagined. Her decision will determine a legacy—not only for Saga, but for the world she never knew she was fated to lead.

So nothing surprises her more than catching the eye of Tyr Fredriksen at her first college party. The imposing Swede is arrogantly charming, stubbornly overprotective, and runs hot-and-cold in ways that defy reason... until Mia learns that she's fallen for the Norse God of War; an immortal battle deity hiding on Midgard (Earth) to protect a valuable Asgardian treasure from a feral enemy. With a price on his head, Tyr brings more than a little excitement to Mia's rigidly controlled life. Choosing Tyr may be the biggest distraction—or the greatest adventure—she's ever had.

Learn more about the world of S.T. Bende at www.stbende.com.

www.ingramcontent.com/pod-product-compliance
Lightning Source LLC
Chambersburg PA
CBHW050513190726

48284CB00003B/794